"I'm just so angry at him right now…"

Mike's voice was terse over the phone. "What do you say I grab some takeout? We can get started on putting this case together for the prosecutor's office."

Christy was intrigued by the thought of spending some time with him. "That sounds nice."

"Great. I'll see you in about an hour?"

She was about to respond when bright lights from a vehicle roared up on her car. She cried out.

"Christy? Are you okay?"

Before she could say anything, the vehicle sped up and rammed the back of her car. "Mike!" she screamed. She turned the steering wheel as the pickup she could now see tried to push her off the road. "Someone's running me off the road!"

"Hold on, Christy. I'm on my way."

She'd been trained in defensive maneuvers, but her little rental car was no match for the oversize pickup.

The truck rammed her again, and this time, she couldn't control it. Her car careened off the road and plowed into a tree.

And darkness pulled her under.

Virginia Vaughan is a born-and-raised Mississippi girl. She is blessed to come from a large Southern family, and her fondest memories include listening to stories recounted around the dinner table. She was a lover of books from a young age, devouring tales of romance, danger and love. She soon started writing them herself. You can connect with Virginia through her website, virginiavaughanonline.com, or through the publisher.

Books by Virginia Vaughan

Love Inspired Suspense

Lone Star Defenders

Dangerous Christmas Investigation
Missing in Texas

Cowboy Protectors

Kidnapped in Texas
Texas Ranch Target
Dangerous Texas Hideout
Texas Ranch Cold Case

Cowboy Lawmen

Texas Twin Abduction
Texas Holiday Hideout
Texas Target Standoff
Texas Baby Cover-Up
Texas Killer Connection
Texas Buried Secrets

Visit the Author Profile page at LoveInspired.com for more titles.

MISSING
IN TEXAS

VIRGINIA VAUGHAN

LOVE INSPIRED SUSPENSE
INSPIRATIONAL ROMANCE

LOVE INSPIRED® SUSPENSE
INSPIRATIONAL ROMANCE

ISBN-13: 978-1-335-63877-9

Recycling programs
for this product may
not exist in your area.

Missing in Texas

Love Inspired
22 Adelaide St. West, 41st Floor
Toronto, Ontario M5H 4E3, Canada
www.LoveInspired.com

Printed in Lithuania

MIX
Paper | Supporting
responsible forestry
FSC® C021394

And I will restore to you the years that the locust hath eaten, the cankerworm, and the caterpiller, and the palmerworm, my great army which I sent among you.
—*Joel* 2:25

For Carter. Adventure awaits you.
I pray God gives you courage and strength
throughout your new journey.

ONE

Little clouds of steam circled the mug of coffee Deputy Mike Tyner's aunt had just poured him. She returned the pot to the stove then sat across from him as she shook her head. "I'm worried about him," she told Mike and he nodded.

"I know, Aunt Peggy." Truth be told, he was worried too.

"Rebecca says he's depressed and hostile. She can't reach him anymore and neither can I. We just don't know what to do."

"I'll talk to him," Mike offered.

His cousin, Cliff Tyner, was a troubled man whose emotional state had steadily gone downhill over the years. Drinking and drug use had only aided his decline.

He wasn't that close to Cliff despite the fact that there was only a few years' age difference between them, but his aunt Peggy had practically raised Mike after his mother had abandoned him and his father worked all the time. She was the one he'd gone to with his needs and worries and she'd always made herself available to him and treated him more like a son than a nephew. Now that he was grown, he would do anything he could to make her life easier, even if it meant dealing with her wayward son.

"I'll go by and speak with Rebecca and see if there's anything I can do for her and the kids."

As he stood, Aunt Peggy hugged his neck. "God bless you, Mike."

He kissed her cheek then headed outside. As he passed through the living room on the way to the front door, he noticed a hole in the wall. She hadn't mentioned that earlier and he hadn't seen it when he'd entered the house. Now the way she'd ushered him quickly into the kitchen when he'd arrived made sense. He turned back to her and motioned to it. "Is that Cliff's work?"

She looked embarrassed but nodded. "He was here last night carrying on. Said someone at the bar brought up the girl and, of course, they got into a fight. He came here before going home and was so worked up he punched the wall." She fiddled with her necklace the way she did when worry overwhelmed her. "I don't think anyone besides her family wants that girl found more than I do."

"I know, Aunt Peggy. Me too."

The Tyner family had been living under a cloud of suspicion for the past twelve years, ever since Cliff's high school girlfriend had gone missing while driving home from college for Christmas break. Cliff had been the prime suspect in her disappearance and Mike had spent years trying to prove his innocence. It didn't help that Mike had been the last-known person to see her alive that night; their chance meeting had made him even more determined to find her. He couldn't help but wonder if he'd missed something in their encounter that might have prevented this tragedy.

He climbed back into his SUV and headed to the sheriff's office. That night was forever ingrained in Mike's memory. He'd been on the job less than a year when he'd seen the little white sedan speeding down the highway and pulled her over. They hadn't been friends but Mike had known her and let her go without ticketing her, instead giving her a warning to slow down. She'd promised to be more careful then thanked him and gone on her way, never to be seen again.

The image of her taillights vanishing into the dark night still haunted him.

His call sign broadcasting over the police radio pulled him from that memory. He radioed into Dispatch.

"Sheriff Thompson wants to see you back at the station," Allison Meeks, the day shift dispatcher told him.

"On my way," he responded.

Checking in on Rebecca and the kids would have to wait. He couldn't ignore a request from the boss herself. It wasn't often he was called to see the sheriff personally, so he couldn't imagine what she could want with him. It felt a little like he was being summoned to see the principal, only he couldn't think of one thing he'd done wrong to warrant it.

He pulled into the parking lot then headed in to see Sheriff Thompson, taking a deep bracing breath before he knocked. She held the phone to her ear with one hand but waved him in with the other. She'd only had the top job for four years, and he'd worked for the previous sheriff as well before he retired, but he'd always considered Sheriff Deena Thompson to be fair and tough on crime. She wasn't known to micromanage and she trusted her deputies to do their jobs. It was something he'd always admired about her.

A photograph of her son sat on a corner of the desk along with other photos of her parents and one of herself with retired Sheriff Murphy as he'd passed the torch to her on election night.

"You wanted to see me, Sheriff?" he asked as she ended her call.

"Yes, Mike. Come on in. I wanted to speak with you about the Dawn Cafferty case."

He grimaced at the mention of that case, the very one his aunt had been lamenting about. Three other investigators before Mike had tried to solve it since it had gone cold and Sheriff Thompson had given him a lot of leeway to investigate on his own time. He prayed she wasn't going to take that latitude from him now and make him put the case aside. He wasn't ready to do that. The answer to what really had happened to Dawn was still out there.

"I want you to have copies made of the file then gather all the evidence and set it all up in the back conference room."

This was new. He lifted his head a little higher as anticipation struck. "Has there been a new lead?" He knew every word of those documents, having studied them in detail over the years, and was excited to learn that she wasn't shutting down the case but opening it back up.

"Not that I'm aware of, but I have been contacted by the FBI. An agent is coming to town to review the case in hopes of making some progress on it."

He shifted in his chair. "Why now, Sheriff? It's been twelve years. The FBI has never been involved before."

She shrugged. "All I know is that an Agent Williams is coming to town to review the file and do what they can to move it forward, and they'll have our full cooperation. This case has been a shadow on our community and this department for too long and I'm personally glad for the help to close it."

"Me too." Excitement filled him. Having the Fed's resources and experience might be a game changer. Only, a part of him was hesitant to hand over control when his family's reputation was on the line. "I'd like to be part of the investigation if I can."

His gut clenched waiting for her response. Solving this case was so important but letting it go wasn't easy. Thankfully, the sheriff agreed. "As far as I'm aware, Agent Williams will be coming alone, so she'll need support from this office. I want you on the case with her. You know that file backward and forward, plus you're familiar with the town. You should be a valuable asset to Agent Williams." She eyed him with hesitation. "That is, if you think you can be objective."

He gave her a determined head nod. "I can. I want this solved."

"Good. She should be arriving in town later this afternoon. Make sure everything is ready by then. This will be your primary duty assignment until further notice."

He thanked her then hurried out to get started. Still excited, he got to work gathering everything together and setting it up. He was glad to have the help to solve this case and excited about working with the FBI. This cloud had loomed over his family for far too long.

Agent Williams might finally be able to do what they hadn't been able to—solve this case once and for all and prove his cousin's innocence.

FBI agent Christy Williams tensed as she made the left turn onto the Mercy Highway. Her eyes watered and she wiped away a tear as she drove on. Had she turned right, she would have been traveling down the last road Dawn was known to have traveled. She would eventually go down that road, but not tonight. She was eager to get to her hotel before launching herself into this investigation.

It was eerie coming to Mercy, Texas, after all these years. Her college roommate, Dawn Cafferty, had vanished twelve years earlier without a trace while making her way home for Christmas break. Somewhere along Mercy Highway was the last spot where Dawn had been seen alive by a patrol officer from the sheriff's department. She'd read through his testimony about how he'd stopped her for speeding but ultimately let her off with a warning. Christy had never questioned that account until a few years ago when she'd discovered the deputy's connection to their main suspect. She couldn't wait to ask him about that. She'd spent her life after college studying this case to the detriment of everything else. Her friends had all married and started families, but not her. She'd focused her life on working and gaining the skills and experience she'd need to solve Dawn's case once and for all and find justice for her friend.

Besides, the fear of messing up again had caused her to keep any potential romantic partners at arm's length.

She drove through town and found her hotel with no problem, checked in, dropped off her bags in her room, then headed for the sheriff's office. The area itself looked quaint and charming, but she saw this community through a different lens. A darkness lurked beneath the surface. One that had never been exposed. She was here to do just that.

Sheriff Thompson greeted her at the front desk when she arrived and Christy followed her to her office. Christy summed up the department as she walked. It wasn't large, but she'd seen smaller. She counted at least a half dozen desks for investigations. Not too shabby. But how many missing-and-murdered cases had these investigators actually performed? She'd worked several during her time with the FBI.

Sheriff Thompson held the door then closed it once Christy had entered the office. She didn't mince words. "I was surprised to hear the FBI was looking into this case. They were never involved in the original investigation and it doesn't have any federal jurisdiction. Plus, it's been cold for years. Why the interest now?"

It was a fair question and she'd determined to be transparent about why she was there. Technically, the FBI didn't have any rights to review this case. They'd never been asked to help. And the sheriff was right. They had no jurisdiction since Dawn had last been seen in the area. "I have to be honest with you. This case has a personal component to it. I knew the victim. Dawn and I were college roommates. Her disappearance has haunted me for years. As to why now? I joined the FBI a few years after college. I've now got nearly a decade of experience under my belt and I feel like I've finally got the skills to try to tackle it. I've read and learned everything I could about this case, but I've never had access to the official case file."

Sheriff Thompson seemed to ponder her response. She had nothing to gain by allowing Christy to reopen this case and the FBI certainly had no authority to do so without her consent. She'd been grateful when the sheriff had agreed to her request.

Finally, she nodded. "I wasn't involved in the original investigation, but I remember the case. Everyone who lives here does. This mystery has also haunted this town. It's gone through multiple investigators throughout the years. It hasn't been forgotten. That's the only reason I approved your request to reopen it. But I can't afford to dedicate many person hours to a case I'm not sure can be solved. I've asked Deputy Tyner to work with you."

She recognized the name. "Deputy Mike

Tyner? Wasn't he the deputy who pulled Dawn over the night she vanished?"

Sheriff Thompson conceded. "It's his connection to this case. He's spent years going through it and probably knows the facts better than anyone else in the office."

"But isn't he related to the main suspect? Does that present a conflict?"

"Not in my eyes. He's honest and open-minded, plus he's determined to find answers. However, if working with him is going to be a problem—"

"No, it's fine," Christy assured her. If the sheriff had confidence in her deputy then she, too, could keep an open mind.

"Okay then. I asked him to set up in the back conference room. I'll have someone show you there."

She listened as the sheriff made a call and then a deputy arrived to escort her. "Thank you for allowing me to do this, Sheriff."

She nodded before turning back to her work. "I hope your fresh eyes find something new."

"Me too."

Her eyes were far from fresh. She'd studied this case extensively, dug up everything she could on the disappearance and the law enforcement response, including using FBI contacts,

Missing in Texas

accessing freedom of information requests, speaking to journalists covering the case and even podcasters who'd dived into the mystery. But she'd never before had access to the all the evidence and case file. To her knowledge, no one except the Mercy County Sheriff's Office had, and they still hadn't been able to crack it.

She followed the deputy to a conference room where she found another deputy, a man she recognized from his photo. Deputy Mike Tyner. The last person to see Dawn alive.

She'd seen his photo many times but it was twelve years old and didn't do him justice. His broad shoulders and square jawline gave him the aura of strength and power, yet his eyes, along with the slight curve of his lips, emitted a kindness about him that she liked.

"Deputy Mike Tyner." He offered his hand to shake and she took it. She sensed no hostility in him toward her, which surprised her. After all, she was there to prove his cousin was a killer.

"Agent Christy Williams. I just met with your sheriff. She said you were going to assist me in reopening this case."

"She's reassigned me temporarily. I think she's hoping to get this case solved so I'll stop obsessing over it." He rubbed the back of his neck nervously. "I'm sure you know my involvement in it."

So, they weren't going to tiptoe around that. Good. "You were the deputy on patrol that pulled her over for speeding, ultimately becoming the last person to see her alive."

"Aside from her killer," he interjected.

"You're also the first cousin of the prime suspect, Cliff Tyner."

"That's right."

He wasn't holding back anything and she liked that. "I understand you've spent years going through this case. I've heard lots of speculation about why, but I'd like to hear your version."

"It's not a secret. This case has hung over my family for years. I spent all this time hoping to prove my cousin's innocence. His life has been overshadowed by these terrible accusations and, in the process, so has the whole family's lives."

He was loyal. It was an admirable trait, one she hoped didn't interfere with her investigation. "Is that the only reason?"

He rubbed his neck again and she could see he was struggling with something. "No. I keep thinking back to that night and wondering what I could have done differently. If I missed something that might indicate what happened to her. I've just never been able to see it."

"Surely you've worked lots of cases where people went missing or were killed. Do you get so emotionally involved in all of them?"

"I've worked some, but this was my first. I was twenty-one and had only been with the sheriff's office for six months. I knew Dawn. At least, I knew who she was. She dated my cousin for years and, although we weren't really close or ran in the same circles, I lived with him and my aunt for years after my dad died when I was in high school."

"So you want to prove his innocence for the sake of your family."

"I want answers. My family needs answers."

She admired his honesty but doubted he really wanted to know the truth. "And if the answers point to your cousin having murdered Dawn, how will that help your family?"

"It won't, because my cousin isn't a killer. I know him. He's got a lot of problems, but I don't see one of them being a killer."

"Look, Deputy Tyner, I can appreciate your loyalty to your cousin, but my job here is to go where the evidence leads me."

"That's fine by me," he told her. "Because my job is to make sure you go where the evidence leads you and not just try to pigeonhole the man you think did this."

So, they were at odds. She mulled that over for a moment then decided it was a good thing. She had come here with the assumption that she knew who'd killed her friend. That wasn't the way an investigation should go. He would keep her from focusing all her attention on Cliff Tyner if a lead took them elsewhere and she would make certain he didn't ignore evidence that implicated his cousin. They could keep one another honest.

"Okay then. Let's get to work." She'd trained herself to read people and she saw honesty in this man. Working with him would be challenging but she thought they would complement one another.

Satisfied, she went about arranging the space for working. "I'd like to take the rest of today to review the case in depth and make a list of priorities. Ideally, I'd like to start conducting interviews by tomorrow afternoon."

He agreed with that and they got to work. He set up an evidence board with all the pertinent information in one place while Christy poured through the documents.

She didn't find any smoking gun within the case file she managed to get through. The in-

vestigative notes were thorough but, unfortunately, there wasn't much evidence indicating
what might have happened to Dawn that night.
No witnesses admitted seeing her after Deputy
Tyner had stopped her and her cell phone had
showed no evidence of calls she'd placed to
anyone. She and her car had simply vanished
into the night.

Or so it seemed. No one ever truly vanished
without a trace.

Their job was to find the trace of evidence
that pointed to what had happened to her.
Christy had already arranged for a colleague
she'd worked with in the FBI, who'd now gone
into private business, to reexamine Dawn's and
Cliff's cell phone data and GPS information.
The police had done this twelve years earlier,
but she hoped new technologies might make
a difference and finally give them a break in
this case.

After several hours of reading, she stood and
stretched. The sheriff's office had cleared out
and quieted down as the night shift took over.
She glanced at her watch and realized it was
after ten. Tomorrow morning would come early
and she was looking forward to starting the interviews. But she needed to be alert to do so.

She didn't want to miss something vital because of a lack of sleep.

Although she hated to leave, it was time to say good-night.

Mike returned several boxes to the evidence room to be locked up for the evening so as not to compromise the chain of custody. When he returned, he picked up the box of files she'd collected and offered to carry it out to her car.

"You don't have to do that," she told him as they left the building.

"I don't mind. Besides, I'm going the same way. Shall I pick up coffee for us in the morning? I usually stop anyway."

"Sure, thank you, Deputy."

"Please, call me Mike."

"Mike." She nodded as she unlocked the car and he loaded the box into the back seat. "See you tomorrow morning, Mike."

He flashed her a smile. "Bright and early."

So far, she liked Deputy Tyner... Mike. She'd expected some hostility from the sheriff's office since she was coming in to solve what they couldn't but, after their initial dustup, she hadn't sensed any further tension between them. If Mike could keep an open mind about his cousin, she could too.

She watched him as he walked to his sheriff's-office-issued SUV. He stopped as he reached it then turned back and waved her way. She quickly started the engine to her own vehicle, her face warming at being caught staring at him. She couldn't deny he was attractive, but she wasn't in town for that. And besides, she'd seen something familiar in Mike Tyner that was a blockade for either of them finding peace. Guilt. It was something they shared in their emotional attachment to the case. Guilt had been Christy's constant companion since she'd learned of Dawn's disappearance. She should have been with her that night and, if she had been, things would have turned out differently. How could she ever find happiness with someone when her friend was still missing?

It was a short ride back to her hotel and it would be hard to get lost. She headed over a small bridge then hit the downtown area. It wasn't exactly booming with activity but there were still plenty of restaurants, businesses and cars on the road even at this time of night.

She turned into her hotel then parked and carried the box of files through the lobby and to the elevator, already thinking about what she was going to order from room service and how good a hot shower would feel on her already tense muscles from traveling then sitting for the afternoon.

She readied her keycard as the elevator doors slid open on her floor. As she neared her room, she hefted the box of files onto her hip then slid the card into the slot and pushed open the door.

Shock rattled through her as she surveyed the sight before her. Her suitcases open and clothes everywhere. Her makeup bag's contents scattered on the bathroom vanity. The carton of files she'd spent years gathering about this case open and papers everywhere.

She dropped the box in her arms. Someone had ransacked her hotel room.

And, pinned to the wall with a knife, was a sheet of paper with one word written on it.

Leave.

The dark underbelly of Mercy had already showed itself.

TWO

Christy searched through her belongings. Nothing appeared to be missing, but the fact that someone had broken into her room and dug through her files on the case was telling. Someone in town had been in her room, trying to figure out why she was in Mercy and, given the threatening note stabbed into her wall, whoever it was wasn't happy with the answer. If they'd meant to frighten her into leaving, they didn't know her that well. This new threat only strengthened her desire to find out who was behind this.

The hotel night manager arrived at her door and introduced himself as Steve Murphy. She'd called down to the front desk to let them know what had happened. He appeared concerned when he surveyed the mess and his eyes widened in surprise when he spotted the knife in the wall. "I'm so sorry this happened. We run a nice hotel. Crime isn't something we usually have to deal with, but don't worry, I've phoned the sheriff's office."

"Don't touch anything," she told him. "I want the sheriff's office to dust for prints." She was hoping there would be some imprints on the knife and paper, and she'd left the door propped open so no one could contaminate it, hoping that the housekeeping staff cleaned the handles regularly so there might be some fresh prints there too. She doubted that was a top priority for the cleaning staff and wasn't confident they would get impressions they could use, but they needed to try.

Mike arrived at the door and she was surprised to find she was glad to see him. Then she remembered he was one of the few people who knew she was in town and why. They'd been together since her arrival, so he couldn't have been involved in the break-in, but who had he told about her investigation?

He surveyed the room then looked at her, his expression full of concern that seemed genuine. "Are you okay? Are you hurt?"

She had to keep her guard up and that meant remaining professional. "I'm fine. I walked in on this. The intruder was already gone."

"Is anything missing?"

"No. Everything is here. It looks like whoever did this was just checking me out. Is this how locals treat out-of-towners?"

His cheeks reddened and his jaw clenched as he spotted the knife in the wall and the threatening note. "No. Absolutely not."

"I'll need to change rooms," she told the night manager, who agreed.

"I'll go make sure we have a room ready for you."

"I can dust for fingerprints myself so we don't have to wait on a forensics team. Let me run down to the car." Mike followed the manager out while Christy started packing up some of her papers that were strewn around. She didn't like knowing that someone had rummaged through her belongings. It was an invasion of her privacy and her personal space, and didn't do much to endear her to Mercy. It wasn't fair to judge an entire community by one person's actions, but she'd been in town less than eight hours and had already been violated and threatened.

Mike returned with a black suitcase that he opened to reveal a fingerprinting kit. She continued cleaning up while he bagged the knife and note as evidence then tried lifting prints from the door, the dresser and the several countertops.

Finally, he gave up. "I can't get a good print from anywhere. Everything is too smudged to lift a clean print."

She was disappointed but not very surprised. "It was unlikely anyway getting prints from a hotel. No telling how many people have been through here."

"I'll let the lab process these," he said, motioning to the evidence bags. "Maybe they'll find something." He put away his kit then walked over to the windows to check them. They didn't budge. "I'll help you move your things to a new room then I want to talk to the night manager. There's no sign of forced entry on this door and the windows don't open, which means someone used a keycard to access the room. There will be an electronic log. The front desk should be able to tell whose card was used to enter and when."

He grabbed her suitcases and his black case with the evidence while she carried her box of files up the elevator to the next floor where the manager had set up a room almost identical to the ransacked one. They dropped her things onto the bed to put away later. Tomorrow, she would go out and buy security cameras for the room as an added precaution. At least then, if someone broke in, she would know who.

She locked her door and followed Mike down the hallway. "It looked like someone was trying to figure out why I was in town, but who would have known I was here and what I was in town to do?"

He sighed and pushed the elevator button. "This is a small town, Agent Williams."

"Christy, please."

"News spreads fast. I found out hours ago that you were coming in to work on this case. I guarantee it was all over town before you even hit the Mercy County limits."

"But why make me a target now? You've been investigating this case for years. Have you been harassed this way?"

His face reddened. "No, but then I haven't made any headway on the case in all these years either. It's possible, assuming this is related to the case, that whoever did this thinks you might do better. Why else would they demand you leave town?"

She hadn't grown up in a small town but she'd worked cases in small towns and knew what he said was true. She'd been a target of the rumor mill since the moment she'd arrived in Mercy. It was eerie to think that people had been watching her and that someone had been determined enough to break into her hotel room and threaten her. The fact that she suspected there was a killer in town only made this break-in even more disturbing.

They walked to the front desk where the night manager keyed up the information. He sighed. "It looks like your room was accessed by one of the housekeeper's keys at eight thirty-six this evening. That key belongs to Stacy Cooper. Only, she wasn't even working at the time, so there was no reason for her to enter. She clocked off duty at four."

"We're going to need to speak with Stacy," Mike told him.

Steve nodded. "I'll call her and have her come in."

It didn't take long for Stacy to arrive at the hotel. She was a petite young woman who appeared worried at the idea of getting into trouble.

Steve explained the situation and she denied entering Christy's room. "I clocked out and left at four then went home. I have to pick up my son after school. We went straight home. I haven't been back here."

"Where is your keycard?" Mike asked her.

"I keep it in my locker with my uniform."

"We're going to need to see it."

She shrugged and they followed her down to

the employee area and a row of lockers. Stacy walked with determination at first, but slowed as they neared the end of the row of lockers.

"What's the matter?" Christy asked her.

She gulped hard. "My locker door is open." She pointed to it and Christy saw one door slightly ajar.

She walked to it and saw that the lock had been forced. She pushed the door open, doing her best not to directly touch it. They could fingerprint that too. Then she motioned for Stacy to find her badge.

The young woman pulled down her uniform, which had been put away neatly on a hanger. She dug through the pocket then her face fell. "It's not here." She rummaged through the rest of her belongings then shook her head. "It's gone. Someone must have taken it."

Christy wasn't surprised. The lock had been pried open, so she didn't even bother asking Stacy if she'd given anyone the combination. If she had, they wouldn't have needed to break in. She didn't sense any deception in the young woman either.

"Can you think of any reason why someone might choose to take your key?" she asked instead.

Stacy shook her head. "I don't know. Everyone who works here knows I work a steady shift, nine to four every weekday. I'm a single mom, so I need a steady schedule."

"Maybe because they knew she wouldn't be back to discover it gone until the morning," Mike suggested.

So, someone had stolen her keycard and broken into Christy's hotel room. They'd had to know it would eventually lead back to her. That was either their plan or else they just hadn't cared. It was also possible the intruder had simply picked a random locker and this had no connection to a specific employee.

"Is there anyone who might have a grudge against you?" Christy asked her. "Someone who might want to see you get into trouble?"

"I don't think so. I get along with everyone."

Steve came to her defense. "Everyone likes Stacy. I can't think of anyone who has a grudge against her that works here."

Mike nodded. "I'm thinking this was just a crime of opportunity."

Christy bobbed her head. "Agreed."

"I've already put a block on that card," Steve said. "Whoever took it won't be able to use it again." He glanced Stacy's way. "Come with me to the office and I'll get you a new keycard to use. I'll also put in an order to replace the lock."

Stacy gathered her things from the locker then left with Steve while Mike got to work dusting the locker for prints. He found two good ones, but Christy wasn't optimistic.

"They probably belong to Stacy. We should make sure we have hers on file to compare them to."

"We do. She worked as a substitute teacher for the school system before she started here full time. She had to be fingerprinted as part of that job."

"You know her?"

He shrugged and gave her a lazy smile. "Small towns. She used to babysit for my nieces."

"Good. Then we shouldn't have any problem figuring out if it's her print on the locker door or someone else's. What kind of person is she?"

"I think she's a good person. I can't see her getting involved in anything like breaking and entering. I know she was thankful to get this full-time job after her husband was killed during a training accident. He was in the military."

"She's a single mom. Maybe she would if she needed the money."

He shook his head. "I don't rule anything out

but, if she was in on it, why not just hand over her keycard and report it stolen."

"Whoever broke into my room wasn't trying to hide that they'd been there. They weren't worried about protecting her, so I'm inclined to believe she's not involved unless we find evidence to the contrary."

He finished up. "I'll take these back to the sheriff's office along with the knife and note. We should know something first thing in the morning."

"Good. I also want to pull up the video feeds for the hotel. Surely there's a camera that caught someone who wasn't supposed to be here."

He picked up his case and they headed back upstairs. Stacy was already gone, headed home to her son, and Steve gave them no blowback when Christy requested to see the video surveillance.

He led them into the office and pulled it up on his laptop. "The cameras mostly cover the parking lot and lobby and the hallways."

She was glad to see there were cameras in the hallways so they could focus on that video feed to see who had approached her room.

A bell rang and Steve glanced out. "I have a customer at the front desk. Be right back."

Christy continued to watch the feed, speeding up the timing until a figure stepped off the elevator and walked down the hallway, stopping at her room. He had broad shoulders and wore jeans and a jacket along with a ball cap pulled low over his head so she couldn't see his face. He also avoided glancing at the cameras, indicating he might know they were there.

"I can't see his face," she said, and Mike shook his head.

"Neither can I."

"He's purposefully not looking at the camera."

They watched as he used a keycard to enter her room. She noted the time. It was the same time Steve had said the card had been used. She noted the time again when he walked out. He'd been inside her room for nearly fifteen minutes. That was a long time to not get caught.

They ran through the video feeds from the lobby and watched him enter the hotel and leave. Neither shot gave them a better look at his face. She changed the feed to the outside cameras, but the figure walked on foot down the street and vanished from view.

"Everything okay in here?" Steve asked when he returned.

"Do you remember seeing this man enter or leave the hotel?" she asked him.

He glanced at the screen and noted the times then shook his head. "No, I didn't see him. I must have either been helping another customer or was in the office at the time."

"Can you screenshot that image for me?" Mike asked, focusing on one of the man entering the lobby. "I can pass it around at the sheriff's office and see if anyone recognizes him." Steve used the screenshot feature and sent it to Mike. Christy heard it ding as he received it. He glanced at his phone. "Got it."

"Will there be anything else?" Steve asked. "I'm in nursing school during the day and am usually able to study for exams here when it's quiet."

"Sure, go ahead," Christy told him. "For now, we have what we need." Although it hadn't produced any solid leads about who had broken into her room and threatened her or why.

She turned to Mike. "I'm going up to my room. I want to be bright and alert for our interviews tomorrow."

He nodded. "I'll drop these by the sheriff's office then head home myself. I'll see you tomorrow."

She watched him go and headed upstairs to her new room. She was glad he'd answered the call about the break-in. She was going to need someone who knew this town if she hoped to break this case and, although she was inclined not to trust anyone in Mercy, so far, Mike seemed to be a good guy.

Mike hurried out to his SUV and climbed inside. He felt embarrassed that this had happened in his town and that it had happened to Christy. Mercy was a nice town. They had their problems, just like any other community, but Mike had always been proud of his hometown.

Until now.

He hadn't expected to connect with the pretty FBI agent the way he had, but he admired her determination to solve this case. It didn't hurt that she was good-looking, too, with her long blond hair and athletic build.

Slow down, Mike.

It didn't really matter whether or not he found her attractive. She would never give him a second look since he was the cousin of the man she suspected of killing her friend. And, even if she did, she would never forgive him for what he'd just done.

He took out his cell phone and stared at the image of the man they'd seen breaking into Christy's hotel room. His first thought had been that it might be Cliff. She hadn't seemed to make that connection, but then, she was working off old photographs of his cousin. He'd been barely eighteen when that photo had been taken. He was thirty now. Christy didn't know how he'd put on weight over the years or that Mike had given him a Texas Rangers ball cap two Christmases ago that he wore faithfully. Sure, he wasn't the only one in town with that hat, but the coat and shoes had looked familiar too.

And he hadn't spoken up about it either. Shame filled him over that. He should have voiced his thoughts to her the moment he'd had them, but she was already hungry to take down his cousin. He wasn't going to hand her the rope until he knew for sure it was him.

It was late at night and he didn't want to disturb Rebecca or the kids, so he decided to wait to call until the morning to confront his cousin.

He slept for a few hours then got up, dressed, shaved and grabbed a cup of coffee to revive him. His mind was still on that photo and he was determined to find out if it had been Cliff who'd broken into Christy's hotel room.

He drove to their house and saw that Cliff's truck was gone from the driveway. He stopped anyway. He'd promised his aunt he would check in on Rebecca and the kids and he'd never had the opportunity yesterday. The front door opened and Rebecca hurried the kids out to catch the school bus. She saw him and waved, motioning for him to come inside. Once there, she had a pot of coffee waiting. He accepted it, having already drained his first cup. It was going to be a "multiple mugs of coffee" kind of day.

"Where's Cliff? I noticed his truck is missing."

She pulled a hand through her hair then gave a weary shrug. "Honestly, I don't even know. He came home late last night, drunk again, and he was ranting and raving. I made him sleep it off on the couch but, when I got up this morning, he was already gone. He's been working the late shift at his job, so I know he doesn't start there until later this afternoon."

"What time does his shift start?"

"He's been working the two-to-ten shift, so I don't generally expect him home until after the kids are put to bed. But last night he didn't show up until nearly two o'clock in the morning."

"What was he upset about last night?"

She shrugged. "The same old thing. That girl that went missing. Someone must have mentioned her again because he was railing about being accused of hurting her."

Rebecca knew Cliff better than probably anyone, so Mike took a chance to question her. "Rebecca, do you think he could have harmed her?"

She glanced at him, surprised by that question. "I married him a few years after she vanished and, if you had asked me then, I would have said absolutely not. I believed in his innocence, Mike."

"And now?"

She shook her head and he saw doubt there. "When he's drinking, he gets out of control. I'll admit I've wondered about that some days when I've seen how he is. If he was drinking that night then…" She hesitated before finally voicing her doubts. "Maybe."

It wasn't the answer he'd wanted to hear but Mike couldn't deny he'd had his doubts over the years, too, especially as Cliff's drinking had escalated. But he'd held on to the fact that the Cliff they knew now wasn't the same person he'd been twelve years ago. He hadn't been drinking back then and they'd been close enough to him to believe in his innocence. He hadn't found any evidence in the years since to change his mind about that.

He made a point to ask if she or the girls

needed anything before he left. She insisted they didn't.

As he climbed into his SUV, he pulled out his cell phone and dialed Cliff's number, surprised when his cousin answered. "Hey, I'm sitting at your house. Where are you?"

"I decided to take an early shift at work. What's up?"

"I need to ask you about something. Where were you at eight thirty last night?"

"At work. Why?"

"I suppose you've heard there's an FBI agent in town looking into Dawn's case?"

He sighed. "Yeah, I've heard."

Mike wasn't surprised that he knew. As he'd told Christy, her arrival was likely well known through the grapevine by the time she'd hit town. "Well, her hotel room was broken into last night. Someone trashed it and left her a threatening note."

"And you think I did it?" His tone turned defensive, as usual.

"I have a photo of the perpetrator and it could be you, Cliff. Just tell me the truth."

He sighed loudly and annoyed. "I was at work last night at eight thirty. I don't even know what hotel she's staying at."

It wasn't much of an excuse since there were

only a few hotels in the area to choose from and Christy's was closest to the sheriff's office.

"So the FBI is trying to pin this on me, aren't they?"

"No, they're trying to find the truth about what happened to Dawn, but, yes, you are still a person of interest."

"Then I guess this is it. Either I'll be cleared or arrested by the time this agent leaves town."

He wasn't wrong yet Mike felt the need to reassure his cousin. "I'm working the case, too, with Agent Williams. I'll make sure she doesn't get tunnel vision where you're concerned."

"Thanks, Mike."

Mike ended the call. He hadn't lied to his cousin, but he didn't feel good about it either. He glanced at the kids still waiting by the curb as the school bus arrived. Despite the rumors around town, Cliff had married a good woman and had a nice family, one Mike even envied, but Agent Williams's arrival in town had just put the pressure on a man who was already on the edge. He hoped Cliff could hang on a little longer and give them time to close this case once and for all.

Only, as a cop, he had to do his due diligence before he could approach Agent Williams and say for certain that it wasn't his cousin who had broken into her room.

He drove by the parts store where Cliff worked and saw they were open. He didn't see Cliff's truck parked there, despite just speaking with him and him claiming to be working. Mike got out, walked inside and asked to talk to Cliff's supervisor.

"What can I do for you?" A man approached him and shook his hand.

"I'm Deputy Mike Tyner of the Mercy County Sheriff's Office. I'm also Cliff Tyner's cousin. Is he working today?"

"Sure. He took a morning shift to cover for another employee who called in sick. He's out on a delivery at the moment."

"Can you confirm that he worked last night?"

"Let me check." He pulled up the time clock program on the computer. "He was clocked in from two p.m. and clocked out at ten thirty."

"So he was here that whole time?"

"Here at the store? No. He does deliveries, so he would have been in and out all evening."

"What about at eight thirty? Can you tell where he was at that time?"

"I can tell you where his delivery van was."

"That'll do."

He clicked on a few keys. "The GPS on the

van shows he made a delivery to the Merck store. He was parked there for thirty minutes during that time frame."

Mike was working out the area in his head. The Merck store was close to the hotel. Close enough that Cliff could have walked to the hotel, ransacked Christy's hotel room, then made it back to his van in plenty of time. "Is it normal for a delivery to take that long?"

He shrugged. "It can be. It really depends on how long it takes the employees to accept the delivery and stock the shelves. If they're busy with customers, then our couriers have to wait on them. They can't leave without the store's employees signing the receipt."

So, he still didn't have a concrete alibi, in Mike's opinion. He couldn't rule out Cliff as being the one who'd threatened Christy and ransacked her hotel room.

THREE

Sleep had eluded Christy. She'd tossed and turned, overexcitement mingled with being on guard for another possible intruder lurking in the hallways. Finally, she'd gotten up and dug through the files, jotting down a list of questions she had and people she wanted to interview. Cliff was at the top of the list. He'd been questioned multiple times before by several different interrogators and, while she didn't question their competency, she would love the chance to take a shot at him.

She brewed a pot of coffee then used makeup to try to hide the dark circles forming beneath her eyes from the lack of sleep. She'd wanted to be alert today but circumstances meant she would have to use caffeine to make that happen.

Mike was already there in the conference room when she arrived at the sheriff's office. On the table was the coffee he'd promised to get. She'd forgotten all about his suggestion but it wouldn't go to waste.

"Good morning," he said, standing to greet her. "Did you sleep okay?"

"Not much," she told him. She was dedicated to finding out what had happened to her friend and she wasn't going to allow lack of sleep, or an intruder in her room, to stop her.

What surprised her was how well Mike looked. He'd left when she'd gone upstairs yet he'd beaten her to the sheriff's office this morning, meaning he couldn't have gotten much sleep himself. It didn't show. His eyes looked bright, he was clean-shaven, smelled fresh and looked…nice.

She removed her notebook from her briefcase and flipped to the notes she'd made this morning. "I made a list of the people I want to interview. Obviously, I need to question Cliff, but I want to have all my facts solidified before I do so I can refute anything he says that I know isn't true." She spotted the way his jaw tensed. That was still a sore subject for him. "I'm not saying he will, but I'll be ready if he does."

He shrugged then started gathering addresses, phone numbers and written statements of those the previous investigators had already interviewed. She and Mike would be revisiting the information collected by them to see if anyone's story had changed or if some new lead might be uncovered.

She glanced over the whiteboard at the names and details they'd documented. It wasn't a large case but everything in her mind still pointed to Cliff Tyner. Suddenly, emotion overwhelmed her. "We don't even have a crime scene." She knew in her heart that Dawn was dead, but knowing where it had happened would have been helpful in bringing her killer to justice.

"We could drive the highway and I can show you the spot where I pulled her over."

She turned to him, stunned she hadn't thought of doing that. It was probably as close to a crime scene as they were going to get on this case. "That's a great idea. I turned onto the highway on my way into town but she would have gone the opposite direction to go to her parents' house."

"My theory has always been that she had car trouble after I left her or she stopped for some other reason and someone else came by and picked her up."

"Has the area built up much in the past twelve years?"

"No. It's surprisingly the same. Dark, long and lonely."

She would have preferred to see it at night the same way Dawn had, but she didn't want to wait and examining the area in daylight might give her a better understanding of the highway and its occupants. "Let's take the files we have and start conducting interviews afterward if nothing else comes up."

He grabbed a stack of accordion folders and carried them out to his SUV.

Mike had agreed to drive and she was glad. She might never know what had happened to Dawn, but maybe this would help her make sense of what could have happened.

She took in the scenery until Mike pulled over and indicated a location. "This is where I stopped her. I was parked up the road on patrol and she passed by. She was doing sixty on a fifty highway, so I turned on my lights and pulled her over. I ran the license plate, but it came up under a different name. I later learned it was registered in her maternal uncle's name. She'd purchased the car from him but never changed over the title. But I recognized her when I approached the window. The back seat of the car was packed up with her belongings from school. She said she was headed home

for Christmas so I told her slow it down and
let her go with a warning."

His story today matched the statement he'd
given during the initial investigation and the
fact that he knew the exact spot where he'd
stopped her twelve years earlier confirmed that
this case had made an impression on him.

They both got out and she looked around.
There were few lights on the highway so, at
night, it would have been dark. Mike had been
correct. This part of the road, devoid of houses
and businesses, was surrounded on both sides
by woods. Dark and lonely was right. This area
was a bad place to break down, if that was what
had happened.

"Did she say anything else?"

"She said she was preoccupied. She was
going to see Cliff to break up with him and
she was nervous how he would respond."

"So she hadn't yet when you saw her?"

He seemed to think about it for a moment
before shaking his head. "I guess she hadn't."

She noted his response. Christy knew and
had told investigators at the time that had been
Dawn's plan. Cliff had maintained through the
years that he hadn't seen Dawn that night, but
here were words from her own mouth from another source claiming she was planning to see

him and end their relationship. That was generally the most dangerous time for a woman.

"Were these woods searched?"

He bobbed his head in confirmation. "Yes, we performed searches all up and down this highway for both her and her car, but we didn't find any sign of her."

Christy soaked in every detail she could think of, but this spot was giving her nothing. There had never been any indication that Mike had been involved. In fact, he'd been cleared early on in the investigation. After all, why come forward claiming he'd stopped her if he'd been the one to harm her? Plus, the guilt that was eating him up over his involvement was clear. "Let's continue down the road."

They got back into his SUV and he kept driving. A few miles along the road, she spotted a convenience store. If Dawn had had car trouble, she could have stopped there for assistance. "Was this here twelve years ago?"

He pulled over and stopped. "Yes, it was. It looks pretty much the same as it did then."

The place didn't look great. The rough pavement, old building and signage and outdated pumps didn't give her a great feel. It didn't seem like an establishment she would stop at if she were driving alone but, if Dawn's little

white sedan had been having mechanical issues, it might have seemed necessary to stop
here.

"Was anyone here questioned in the original
investigation?"

"Yes, the store's owner and his daughter
were both questioned, plus the sheriff's office canvassed all along this highway. If they
came across anyone with information, someone would have taken down their statement."

She knew that wasn't necessarily true. The
deputies canvassing might not even have
known what would constitute a lead, but there
should have been a list of people who'd been
spoken to somewhere in the file. They were
only a few miles past the last location Dawn
had been seen, so this gas station should have
been a logical choice to check out. "What do
you know about this store?"

"It's owned by John Bass. He's owned it for
forty years and still works the day shift, but
I believe his son, Conner, works it at night.
They have a deli that serves a good hot lunch
and attracts people from all over the county,
but at night the clientele changes. There's a bar
not far from here that doesn't attract a great
crowd though they do a lot of business. The
sheriff's office has been called there multiple

times for brawling and fights getting out of hand. This station has been robbed quite a few times, too, at night. I think that's why John stopped working the night shift. He's gotten older and thought his son could defend against the rougher crowd better than he could. More of an appearance of strength. It must be working because the calls have gotten fewer over the years. Conner seems to know how to handle himself."

"Why not just close down at night?"

He shrugged. "I suppose they do good business and don't want to lose it."

"What about the time when Dawn went missing? Who was working then?"

He rubbed his neck as he thought about that. "Conner hadn't joined the business yet so John was on duty. I know a deputy questioned him during the initial search for Dawn. There's a copy of his statement in the file—I'll have to find it—but he basically said he didn't see her."

In her experience with cold cases, reinterviewing witnesses was sometimes helpful. "Let's go question him again. His son might have heard something too in the intervening years."

He drove up to the front door and parked. They both got out but a sign on the door stating it wouldn't open for another hour stopped them from entering. Mike peered through the window. "I don't see anyone."

And there were no cars in the lot yet. She nodded and jotted down the names John and Conner Bass. "I'll want to reinterview them both. Hopefully, one of them remembered something more about that night."

"I'll add them to the list, although they're both stand-up guys, and John has a daughter who was only a few years older than Dawn. I'm sure that, if he'd remembered something more, he would have called when the sheriff's office was asking for tips."

"I've interviewed many people who claimed to have called into a tip line but their information was never recorded. It happens more than you think. People are busy or overwhelmed and it just gets lost." She'd even been privy to a few instances where the police department had just disregarded a tip because it hadn't fit with the narrative they'd decided on.

Mike must have sensed she was implying that his office didn't do their job because she saw his face redden. "I was one of the people manning those tip lines. We took down all the information that was called into us. Besides, wouldn't discovering that Dawn did show up here and something happened to her invalidate your belief that my cousin harmed her?"

"I told you I'm open to all possibilities. It just seems that your cousin's involvement is the mostly likely. Dawn confided in me that he had a temper and, statistically, women are in the most danger when they're ending a relationship. That was what she was coming to town to do. It might be that after interviewing the Basses, we discover she did stop here for help and Cliff came and picked her up."

"Then where's her car?"

There were a lot of things that didn't add up in this case and he knew it. This line of conversation would only end up in an argument over whose theory was the right one. They couldn't let this investigation become divided if they hoped to find answers.

"Let's keep going, but I would like to interview John and Conner regardless."

He didn't press the issue. Instead, they both got back into his SUV and he peeled out of the parking lot. The road was barren for miles and, without streetlights, it would have been dark and scary. Christy could imagine a scenario where Dawn went off the road and couldn't get her car back out.

"Is it possible she lost control of the car and

went into the woods somewhere through here?" she asked him.

"Anything is possible, but we didn't find any evidence of brush or trees disturbed for miles, and no one found any evidence of skid marks that might indicate she tried to stop herself. We conducted searches of the woods, too, but found nothing."

Plus, in that scenario, she could have walked the highway to the Basses' store or gotten turned around, lost in the woods and died of exposure. It wasn't impossible that her body hadn't been found given the isolated area and animal activity, but it did seem unlikely. Also, there should have been evidence of the car going off the road that the sheriff's office would have noticed. The off-the-road theory seemed unlikely.

"I know you don't believe your cousin was involved, so what do you think happened to her, Mike?"

He shrugged. "I've seen a lot of bad things in my time with the sheriff's office. A lot of bad people. I've always suspected either she had car trouble or stopped for some reason and the wrong person came by and picked her up."

She tossed his question back to him. "Then where is her car?"

He sighed. "I don't know. We contacted all

the local tow truck drivers back then and no one reported picking up her or her car that night."

"It might be worth reinterviewing them too," she said. "Another thing that's bothered me is why she didn't call for help. If she had car trouble, why not phone someone?" She'd always suspected Dawn had called Cliff for help, but neither of their phone records had showed that to be true. Before she'd come to Mercy, Christy had sent both Dawn's and Cliff's cell phone data to a friend of hers who'd worked for the FBI. She hoped more updated and sophisticated technology that the sheriff's office hadn't had access to twelve years ago might produce new information, and her friend was an expert at cell phone analysis.

"There are a lot of places out here where you can't get a good signal. It's possible she tried but couldn't get through," Mike explained.

He glanced at his side mirror and his jaw clenched. His fingers gripped the steering wheel tighter and she sensed the atmosphere between them change.

"What is it? What's wrong?" She looked in the side mirror and spotted a truck behind them. "Do you recognize that vehicle?"

"It was behind us as we pulled into the

Basses' parking lot. He should be miles down the road by now."

She gulped, understanding his meaning. "They're following us."

She turned in her seat to look out the back. It was definitely a pickup behind them, but it wasn't close enough to get a good description of it or to see the driver. "Why would they be following us?" She thought of the knife in her hotel room and the note threatening her to leave town. Was this more intimidation?

"I don't know, but I'm going to find out. Hang on."

Suddenly, Mike swerved on the road and made a hard turn, changing the SUV's direction so they were heading the other way. He slammed on the gas and zeroed in on the truck.

It, too, made a sharp turn and took off in response.

Mike turned on his sirens and pressed the gas again, closing the distance between them. Christy pulled her gun. If they caught up with the truck, she would be ready to confront whoever was driving. If they were following them, she also wanted to know why and if they'd had any hand in threatening her at the hotel.

The pickup made a sharp turn and disappeared down another road. Mike slammed on the brakes then turned as well, but the road ahead of them now was empty. He kept going, searching several back roads until they ended up on the Mercy Highway. The truck was gone. They'd lost it.

He pounded his hand against the steering wheel then pulled over at a rest stop that consisted of a small building with his and hers bathrooms and a vending machine. A few picnic tables lined the grassy areas but they looked old and weatherworn.

She glanced around and saw minimal lighting. "I'd hate to break down here at night."

"More than you know. This place has a reputation as a place to buy and sell drugs." His face lit up. "Actually, that gives me an idea to follow up on."

"What's that?"

"This place was a hotspot for drug hookups even twelve years ago and I think I have an idea of who might help us decipher who could have been dealing from here the night Dawn disappeared. It might be the lead we've been searching for."

Mike couldn't believe he hadn't thought about this earlier. Like any small town, Mercy had its share of drugs and the rest stop had been a major hub of drug activity twelve years ago. The sheriff's office had eventually cleared the area out, but reports indicated it was becoming popular again.

"What are you thinking?" Christy asked him.

"If memory serves, there was a big drug bust at the rest stop a year or two after Dawn went missing. The leader of the gang dealing from there was arrested and spent some time in prison. If we can track him down, or members of his gang, maybe one of them remembers Dawn showing up that night."

"If what you're saying is true, then she might have stumbled across a drug deal and was killed so she couldn't be a witness. But why would they admit to it?"

"Loyalties change. Maybe someone will confess to it. At the very least, they might say they saw her but she drove off or, if they saw her with someone, they might tell us."

She nodded and entered notes in her book. "It's a good idea. Do you think you can find the case files?"

"I'm hoping Deputy Sabrina Harris can help us. She's worked narcotics for the past five years and she worked with the previous detective. She keeps up with the major players in the area. I'm hoping she can lead us down the right path."

They reached the sheriff's office and got out. They hadn't even discussed the truck that had been following them and Mike still couldn't believe he'd let it get away. But there was no point in dwelling on it when they had a good lead to follow.

Mike led her inside to Sabrina's desk. A photo of her son and her and her new husband, Jake, on their wedding day sat on the edge of the desk, but her inbox was overflowing.

She saw them approach. "Hey, Mike, what's up?" He filled her in on their reopening the cold case investigation. "I heard. I hope you solve it. That mystery has lingered over this town for too long. What can I do for you?"

"We were driving the route Dawn might have driven and noticed the rest stop off the Mercy Highway. Wasn't there a major drug player operating from there around the time?"

She nodded. "That sounds familiar. Deputy Henry was running the show around that time I believe. I can check out his notes. Thankfully, they're all digitalized." She hit a few keys then skimmed through the report. "It looks like a drug king named Tony Freely was running the gang at the time." She read something then shook her head. "Paul Creed was the informant who turned Freely into the police."

He recognized that name. Sabrina and Jake had taken down Creed and his supplier months ago. "Paul Creed? Isn't he dead?"

She nodded again. "Yes, he is. But it looks like he turned on Freely then worked his way up to take over the gang and grow it into the operation Jake and I took down six months ago."

"What happened to Freely?" Christy asked her.

"He went to prison." She clicked on another link and pulled up his rap sheet. "He served an eight-year sentence, but he's been in and out of trouble since then. He's currently a person of interest in a string of convenience store robberies, according to the flag on his record, but there are no open warrants on him so, even if you can find him, you can't compel him to come in for questioning."

"Is there an address for him? He might know something about Dawn."

She jotted down an address on a sticky note and handed it to Christy. "This is his last-known address, but it's over a year old."

"It's at least a place to start. Thanks."

Mike also thanked her and they left the

building, climbing back into his SUV and heading to the address on file for Tony Freely.

He was excited and hoped this could be a break in the case. He couldn't believe it had never occurred to him before. They neared the address Sabrina had given them. It wouldn't be unusual for Freely to have moved, but at least they had a last-known location and a name. They could find him if they needed to. How cooperative he might be was another issue because Sabrina was right. They couldn't force Freely to talk to them and they had nothing to incentivize him to either.

The house they approached was run-down and looked in need of repair. The neighborhood was littered with similar residences. Rusted tools in the yard suggested that someone had been working on a vehicle and hadn't bothered to clean up after themselves.

Mike was on alert and he could see Christy was, too, as they exited the SUV and walked toward the house. He scanned the area for any indication of trouble but the neighbors were quiet this time of day.

Christy knocked on the front door then stepped back, a habit all law enforcement was trained to do in case of conflict.

Mike listened as movement sounded from

inside. Someone was approaching the door. Suddenly, the footsteps stopped and he heard another sound through the thin door. The cocking of a gun.

"Get down," he yelled, diving and tackling Christy. They both hit the ground as a spray of bullets ripped through the door where they'd just been standing.

They had come here looking for answers but it looked like they were going to get a fight instead.

FOUR

The sound of gunfire was deafening. Mike rolled off her, reaching for his gun while she did the same. He grabbed his radio and called in for backup at this address.

"Sheriff's Office! Hold your fire!" he yelled but was doubtful the shooter could hear him over the sound of bullets.

Christy crawled to the side of the house and leaned against the wall. "FBI," she called out. "Put down your weapon and come out with your hands raised."

The gunfire ended and a man stepped out, still holding an automatic weapon.

"Drop it!" Mike yelled over the pounding of his pulse in his own ears.

The man saw them and quickly dropped the gun. He held up his hands. "I didn't know it was cops."

Christy crawled to her feet and hurried over to him as Mike covered her. She kicked the gun out of the shooter's reach then pulled his hands behind him and cuffed him. "You were expecting someone else?"

She read him his Miranda rights as the backup finally arrived then handed him off to another deputy to take back to the station.

Mike's heart was still racing as he watched her morph into action to take Freely into custody. He admired her quick response. Maybe she was used to being shot at, but he wasn't. It took him a minute to process what had just happened.

He glanced at the front of the house. The automatic weapon had practically disintegrated the door and front of the house. He shuddered. That had been too close. He walked to where Christy was leaning against a cruiser. She was pale, strands of her blond hair had come free from its ponytail and she was visibly shaking. Guess she wasn't as formidable as she'd seemed moments ago.

"Are you okay?"

She took in a deep breath then exhaled it to settle herself. "I'm not hurt, but I really wasn't expecting that. It definitely got my adrenaline pumping."

"I wasn't expecting it either. He said he didn't know he was shooting at the police. I wonder who he thought he was firing at."

"It doesn't matter." She pulled her pony-tail out and her hair fell across her shoulders. Her mouth settled in a firm line as she pushed away any residue of fear from what had just happened. "Let's get him back to the department and into an interview room. I can't wait to ask this guy questions and, if he knows what's good for him, he'll answer them."

He didn't envy Freely or anyone who faced her questioning. She was back to being formidable.

He left another deputy in charge of processing the scene and gathering evidence of the shootout. Tony Freely was looking at serious prison time for shooting at law enforcement. Mike followed the car with the prisoner back to the station and, once there, led Tony Freely through the sheriff's office and booked him into the jail. Once he was processed, he took Freely to an interrogation room.

"Is he ready?" Christy asked him as she approached the window that looked into the room.

She'd brushed her long hair and freshened her makeup, and her hands seemed steadier than they had an hour ago right after the shooting. He didn't blame her for being shaken by the incident. He'd been too. It wasn't every day, even in law enforcement, that someone shot at him. He was glad Freely had dropped his weapon and given up on his own without one of them having to take him out. That would have only made a bad situation even worse.

"He's ready," Mike answered.

He was a little nervous to let her take the lead since he didn't really know her style, but she was heading up this investigation. He would follow her lead on the questioning. They had Freely on attempted murder of two law enforcement officers as well as several other charges including a felon with a weapon. If he had any hope of getting out of this without spending the rest of his life in prison, Freely was going to need to cooperate with them.

But he knew career criminals like Freely. He'd been in and out of prison since he was a teen and was used to handling law enforcement and probably knew the law and procedures as well as Mike did. Mike hoped he would be cooperative, but he hoped even more that he had something to bargain with. If he had no knowledge of Dawn to offer, then this had all been for nothing.

Freely was defensive from the start. "Look, I didn't know you were the cops."

"Who did you think you were shooting at?" Mike asked him.

He shrugged. "I've got a price on my head by one of my old subordinates. I thought you were an old rival coming to kill me and I wasn't going down without a fight."

"Then it looks like we just saved your life. Answer our questions and I'll see what we can do about getting you a private cell."

"If this is about those convenience store robberies, then you're wasting time. I wasn't involved."

Christy sat down and Mike took the chair beside her. "This isn't about the robberies." She opened a file and pushed a photo of Dawn in front of him. "We're reopening the case of Dawn Cafferty. She went missing twelve years ago somewhere along the Mercy Highway. I understand you used to work out of that highway rest stop near there."

He shook his head. "I didn't have anything to do with that girl going missing."

"Do you remember the case?"

"I remember seeing it on the news, but I wasn't involved."

"You were working that rest stop at the time, right?"

"Yeah, we worked out of there."

"Do you remember if she stopped there

that night? Maybe she saw something that she shouldn't have seen?"

He shook his head. "No, nothing like that happened."

Mike leaned forward. "But you remember that night, Tony. Something must make you remember it. If you didn't know her, then why does that night stand out to you?"

"Because two of my men tried to kill me that same night. They shoved me into a car and said they were taking over the business. They drove me out to the middle of nowhere, but I got the gun away from one of them and managed to fight back."

Mike jotted down a note to double-check for any unsolved murders or shootouts the night Dawn had gone missing. He'd checked that out before and he had a vague memory of a car that had been found shot up out near the old sawmill. They'd never found any bodies, though, and had never linked it to any other crimes.

"Sounds like self-defense to me," Mike told him. "What were their names and what did you do with their bodies?"

"I didn't kill them. Saw them both the next week. One had a gunshot wound to the leg and was hobbling around on crutches. The other was beaten up pretty good. They lived, but they never tried to take over again. I was watching the news to see if I was being sought for that and I saw the coverage about the girl that went missing. That's why I remember what I saw that night."

"So you did see something." Christy leaned forward, her body stiff in anticipation.

"I didn't see her at the rest stop, but when I was being held at gunpoint in the back seat of my own car, we passed a truck parked on the side of the road. I saw her there with a man. He was trying to push her into the cab of the truck."

"What did he look like?" Christy asked. He felt anticipation rolling off her.

"A big guy. Built like a football player and wearing a ball cap, so I couldn't see much of his face."

That described Cliff to a tee. Mike jotted down something on his notepad just to cover his reaction but Christy shot him a look that said she was thinking the same. "What about the truck?"

"Black with a silver toolbox on the back."

Mike grimaced. His cousin had driven a pickup like that, still did, but so did at least a dozen guys he'd known back then.

"You said he was trying to push her into the

truck," Christy continued. "Did it appear like he was trying to force her?"

"Yeah. He looked mad as all get-out and she was fighting him."

"Do you believe you could point this guy out of a lineup?"

He shrugged. "It's been a while but, at the time, when this was being covered all over the TV and her boyfriend was begging for her return, I remember thinking it was him that pushed her into that truck and that he knew exactly what happened to her."

Christy shot Mike an angry look and he leaned forward. "You're saying it was the boyfriend you saw push her into his truck?" He dug through the files and produced the photo of Cliff.

Freely looked at it, his head moving up and down. "Yeah, that's him."

Mike's stomach hit the floor. Freely had identified his cousin and the truck he still owned. However, all the TV coverage at the time could have clouded his identification too.

"You never told anyone this?" Christy asked him. "You never called into the tip line?"

"No. I had my own worries with the law. I didn't want them to find out about the shoot-out and, at the time, I didn't know if those boys were dead or alive. Besides, I had warrants out for me at the time."

Christy gathered her papers together and stood. "Thank you, Mr. Freely. Someone will be in to take you back to your cell."

"What about my deal?" he demanded.

"If your information works out, we'll talk to the district attorney on your behalf."

Mike stood and joined her then arranged to have Freely returned to a cell until his arraignment hearing.

He saw Christy was livid. Her body was stiff and she was tense. She walked to the conference room and started digging through files. "I need to find out what kind of vehicle Cliff Tyner had registered twelve years ago," she told him.

"Don't bother," Mike said. "I know what he was driving then. A black pickup with a toolbox on the back, just like Freely described."

She slammed her palm against the table in anger. "So he did abduct her that night. He's been lying to everyone all these years. Freely's description matches that of your cousin perfectly." She pulled out the photo of him. "At least, what he looked like twelve years ago."

But Mike wasn't ready to completely concede Cliff was involved. "This guy Freely is a known criminal. He's got a rap sheet longer

than my arm for drugs, guns and violent behavior. He even admitted to having a shootout
the night she vanished, plus, he nearly killed us
today. I'm not sure his credibility is the best."

"No, but at least it's a start. We have an eyewitness that remembers seeing your cousin on
the side of the road arguing with Dawn and trying to push her into his vehicle the night she
vanished. And he has a very plausible reason
for recalling it so vividly as his life was in danger at the time."

"We have the word of a convicted felon who
is facing even more prison time for firing on
a sheriff's deputy and a federal agent. I have
questions like how Cliff knew she was there.
Neither of their cell phone data shows they
were texting or calling one another to meet up."

He'd thought that would be a sticking point
but she only smiled.

"I had a friend of mine who used to work
at the Bureau who analyzes cell phone data
and GPS information take another look at both
Dawn's and Cliff's data. There are updated
methods today that might shed some more light
on that information." She pulled out her cell
phone. "I think I'll call him now and see if he
has anything."

She walked out of the room to make the call

and left Mike to look through the files. He sighed as he rechecked the truck Cliff had driven at the time. The sheriff's office had impounded it, taken photos and done forensic testing. They'd found Dawn's hair and DNA inside the cab of the pickup, but Cliff had always insisted it was from before that night. They had been dating for years and she was known to have been inside the truck on previous occasions. No blood evidence had been found or anything that indicated he'd harmed her inside it. Mike had always stood on that and the cell phone evidence to believe in his cousin's innocence.

The problem was Freely had seemed genuine in his statement. Mike hadn't detected any deception, but then again the guy was a known criminal with plenty of experience lying to the cops. They couldn't take his statement as one hundred percent accurate.

Still, it gave him enough pause to want to talk to his cousin again about his movements that night.

Christy listened as her call to Charlie Summers rolled over to voicemail. Shoot. She'd been hoping he would have answers for her. This new information about Cliff Tyner had lit a fire inside her. It was information the local police hadn't had previously. But Mike was right. Freely's credibility was questionable and she would love some corroborating evidence to back it up.

She walked toward the conference room where Mike was digging through files. He was shaking his head and breathing heavily as he riffled through the reports. She could tell Freely's statement had hit him hard. All the evidence so far was pointing at his cousin.

Then she realized she'd promised him not to get tunnel vision where his cousin was concerned.

Despite this new witness, they still had a lot of investigating to do. She walked into the conference room and stared at the evidence board, an idea brewing. "Does the sheriff's office have any unsolved cases or other women who've gone missing or were killed?"

Mike nodded, reached into a box, grabbed a handful of files and handed them to her. "The only unsolved case that even remotely matched Dawn's at the time of her disappearance was twenty-year-old Denise Fields. She vanished two years before Dawn, but her body was eventually located in a wooded area."

Christy glanced through the files. Denise had been of a similar age and appearance to

Dawn and, according to her file, her boyfriend at the time had been the prime suspect.

"Unfortunately, forensics didn't give us anything to conclusively identify her killer, but one of her friends insisted Denise was intent on leaving him…"

"Which is usually the most dangerous time for a woman," Christy said, finishing his thought.

"True. The only problem was that his family members gave him a solid alibi, so either they were lying and covering for him—"

"Or else he didn't do it."

Christy's instincts were telling her the boyfriend was likely the culprit but since they didn't have any solid evidence to prove that, she taped Denise's photo and information onto the whiteboard as a possible connection to Dawn's case.

"Is she the only unsolved case?"

Mike shook his head. "Since Dawn's disappearance, we've had two more women who've gone missing." He handed her a file. "Carla Denton, fifty-nine years old, reported missing by her best friend, who stated Carla believed that her son and daughter-in-law were plotting to get her. Her keys, identification and vehicle were left behind but no sign of her has been found in the past three years."

Christy scanned the file. The difference in

her age compared to Dawn's, plus the fact that her car wasn't missing, also made Christy believe it wasn't connected, but she put it on the board anyway, along with a big question mark beside her name.

"The final unsolved case is a forty-two-year-old woman named Shirley Morton. She disappeared six years ago, leaving behind a job she loved, a bank account that hasn't been touched and grandkids who, according to family and friends, were the light of her life. Everyone agreed that she would never voluntarily leave. The sheriff's office investigators weren't able to make a determination about what happened to her, but they tended to believe she'd likely had a medical event that incapacitated her and she and her vehicle just have not been found."

It wasn't an unreasonable conclusion given that, according to her family, she'd suffered from known heart-related health issues. Yet, without a body or her vehicle, there was no way to know for certain whether or not she'd been a victim of foul play.

Christy printed off a photo of each woman, along with Dawn's, then taped them all to a whiteboard in the conference room where they were working. She jotted down the details of each case. She would look into each then determine if there were enough dots to connect to Dawn's case. She hadn't come to Mercy to investigate every missing persons case, but doing this would narrow down whether or not they were dealing with an isolated event in Dawn's disappearance or a pattern of behavior.

"Only four open cases of killed or missing women. That's impressive for a county this size," she told Mike.

He nodded. "The majority of our crimes are drug-or domestic-related. Plus, we have good investigators. That's why these missing cases are so frustrating. You just know there has to be an answer out there that we haven't found yet."

She understood the frustration he was talking about. She'd felt it many times in her own efforts to solve Dawn's case. But now she had direct access to the investigators' notes and records, something she'd never had previously and that no reporter or podcaster who had focused on Dawn's disappearance had had access to either.

"Shirley Morton's daughter still calls the office to see if there's been any updates on her mom's case. They're still holding out hope that she's out there somewhere." He stood and tapped Carla Denton's photo. "On the other hand, we never hear a word from her family, which makes me even more convinced that they were involved in whatever happened to her." He glanced at Dawn's photo. "I see Mr. and Mrs. Cafferty around town sometimes and he calls in once a year on the date of her disappearance for an update." He sighed and turned to her. "Hopefully, we'll have news to tell them soon. I imagine they were happy to learn that you were coming to town and reopening their daughter's case."

Christy bit her lip and pretended to be reading through the file on Shirley Morton.

She could see Mike's stern expression from the corner of her eye. "Christy, you did talk to the Caffertys, right? They knew you were coming into town?"

She looked at him and had to admit the truth. "No, I haven't spoken to them."

His jaw dropped and he pushed a frustrated hand through his hair. "You said you and Dawn were college roommates. I assumed you were in touch with the parents."

"We were roommates, but I only met her parents once or twice."

"We have to go and talk to them and let them know we're looking into her case again. They'll want to know."

She nodded in agreement, understanding he was right. Dawn's parents deserved to know they were working on the case. But she'd been dreading this meeting ever since deciding to come to Mercy.

He pulled out his cell phone. "I'll call them and tell them we're on our way over. Okay?"

She glanced at him. For the sake of the case, she needed to do this.

But how was she ever going to face the Caffertys knowing how she'd let down their daughter?

Christy was a nervous wreck as Mike pulled into the driveway of the Cafferty home. She hadn't spoken a word to Dawn's parents in years and she'd been dreading this moment ever since she'd decided to reopen this case.

Mike must have noticed because he turned to her. "Everything okay?"

She bit her lip as the uncertainty overwhelmed her. "I've been trying for so long to look into this case and to find their daughter. Now that we've reopened the file, what if I can't do it? What if I get their hopes up only to have them dashed again? I'm not sure I can face that." She wiped away a stray tear that fled from her eye.

This case meant so much to her, but not nearly as much as it meant to her parents.

"Hope isn't a bad thing, Christy. I've spoken with Mr. and Mrs. Cafferty several times over the years. All they want is to know what happened to Dawn. They would rather take the chance of not finding her than to stop trying."

Mike reached across the seat and touched her arm. She liked the strength of his hand and the reassurance he offered her. It was difficult to face these parents after the way she'd let down their daughter but, with Mike's help, she could face it.

She sucked in a breath and pulled herself together then offered a nervous laugh. "Sorry about that. I think I had a moment of panic there. It's just that this case means so much to me."

He nodded. "I know."

She glanced around at the simple one-story ranch home. It was nice without being fancy. The lawn was bustling with greenery and the front porch had work boots by the door and rocking chairs. This looked like a nice home to grow up in. Dawn had been so keen to get away from it, but Christy now thought that had had more to do with her wanting her independence or getting away from Cliff than anything to do with her family.

She followed Mike onto the porch where he opened the screen door then knocked. Minutes later, a woman opened the door. Christy recognized her from her photos and from seeing her during the searches years ago. She looked older but Christy saw the same smile that she'd shared with her daughter.

"Come on inside," she told them with a heavy Texas drawl. "We've been expecting you."

Christy walked inside then let Mike handle the introductions. "Mr. and Mrs. Cafferty, this is Special Agent Christy Williams of the FBI. She's in town to take a look at Dawn's case."

Mrs. Cafferty's eyes widened. "It's true then? The FBI is looking into Dawn's disappearance?" She put her hands over her heart as tears formed in her eyes. "It's an answer to prayer, isn't it, Lyle?"

She glanced over at the man she was speaking to. Also an older and more worn version of the man she remembered and had seen pictures of. He'd spoken so emotionally raw about his missing child to the press that Christy had cried herself to sleep over her own culpability in the case.

"I actually knew your daughter," Christy told them. She didn't want any lies or secrecy to affect this case. "We went to college together."

Mrs. Cafferty stared at her then smiled. "Of course. You were her dorm mate. I remember you. You've grown into a very beautiful woman."

"Thank you." The pain in her face was obvious as it was clear she was thinking of her own daughter who hadn't had the opportunity to grow into the beautiful woman she should have been.

"Why don't we sit down? Can I offer either of you something to drink? Mike, iced tea? Coffee?"

"No, thanks, Mrs. Cafferty. I'm fine."

"Me too," Christy told her.

She took a seat in an armchair next to Mike's while the couple took the couch. Christy opened her notebook and tried to gather her thoughts. She'd expected this interview to be difficult, but this was excruciating.

"What made you join the FBI?" Mrs. Cafferty asked her.

Christy told her the truth. "It was this case. I wanted to solve it. I wanted to find out what happened to my friend. I thought that by joining the FBI, I could gain the experience to finally figure it out."

Her look seemed to acknowledge that her daughter's disappearance had impacted so many. "I pray you do."

She got down to business. "I know you've been through these questions before with Mike and with previous investigators—"

"We don't mind repeating it," Mr. Cafferty said. "Not if it helps to find her and bring her home."

"Dawn left school at six p.m. I know because I watched her drive away. But she never made it here to the house. We know she arrived in Mercy. She was pulled over just after ten that night. Did she call you to let you know she was running late?"

"No. I wasn't expecting her until the next morning, so we didn't raise the flag until the next day. I tried to call her dorm and spoke to her roommate—you, I guess. That's when I learned that she'd actually left the previous evening. That's when I knew something was wrong."

"Did she ever mention any boyfriends other than Cliff Tyner?"

Mrs. Cafferty smiled sheepishly. "I think you would probably have known better about that than we would have, Agent Williams."

Christy's face warmed. She'd had a conversation with the police at the time about that very subject and they all knew it. Dawn had flirted with a lot of boys but had stayed faithful to Cliff until she could break off the relationship. "Please, call me Christy. I know what I told the police at the time, but I was wondering if she'd told you any different."

Mrs. Cafferty shook her head. "When I would ask how she was doing and if she was seeing anyone, she would always insist that she was in love with Cliff and would never cheat on him." She sighed. "Honestly, I tried to encourage her to stretch her wings a bit. We wanted her to explore new relationships." She glanced at Mike. "No offense to your cousin, but I never wanted her to limit herself to her high school beau. Life is too big for that. At least, it should have been."

"No offense taken," Mike assured her.

"So she never talked to you about anyone else?"

Mrs. Cafferty shook her head. "No one. Telling me about a new boy would have probably meant admitting I was right. That wasn't Dawn's style."

"Did she ever mention any trouble she was having with her car?"

"No. She was home for Thanksgiving and Lyle gave that car a tune-up."

He leaned forward to join the conversation. "I always made sure her car was in good running condition. I didn't want to put her in a bad situation." His voice cracked. "I know what it can be like on these dark back roads."

It was a difficult conversation to get through but Christy managed to ask all of her questions. There were no big revelations and her parents' statements hadn't changed since their initial interviews twelve years earlier. It was obvious they'd loved their daughter and were devastated by her loss. Time hadn't changed that.

Christy ended the interview then stood to shake their hands. "Thank you for taking the time to see me."

Mrs. Cafferty grabbed her hands and pulled her into a hug. "I've been asking God for all these years to send someone who could help us find her. Now, He's brought you. I'm praying you're the one who is going to solve this. I think having a personal interest is going to be your edge."

Her pulse sped up at the added pressure. She'd dealt with emotional families during her time with the FBI, but this was personal and it hit her harder than the others. "I'm going to do my best to figure this out, Mrs. Cafferty. I want to give you the answers you deserve."

The tears threatened her again as she walked outside and took in the view of the place where

Dawn had spent her growing-up years. Christy's perception of this place had been colored by Dawn's adolescent desire to break free from her family, but she'd grown to realize that was just her desire for independence expressing itself. Her folks seemed like nice people who had truly loved her and this looked like a nice place to call home.

She was ready to get out of that house and all the memories it provoked of her friend, but she wasn't yet ready to leave. She walked down to the lake situated behind the residence and Mike followed her. "Are you okay?"

Christy wiped away tears that streamed down her face. "Remember I told you she was my college roommate?"

He nodded and rubbed the back of his neck. "I do."

She turned to him, finally ready to let him in on the terrible truth she'd been holding on to for twelve long years. "Here's something you probably didn't know. I was supposed to come with her to Mercy that night. I had promised her that I would go home with her at Christmas and be there with her while she broke up with Cliff. She said she needed me to be there to be strong for her or else she would wimp out."

Understanding dawned in his expression. "But you didn't come, did you?"

Tears threatened her but she would let them loose. "No. The day before we were supposed to leave, a boy I liked at the time invited me to go to Arizona to spend Christmas with him and his family and I said I would. I was more interested in spending my Christmas by the pool than I was in being there for my friend. Dawn was furious at me for breaking my promise. That's why she left and went home early. I just keep thinking that if I had gone with her as I'd said I would, she might still be here." She covered her face with her hands to help hold back the emotion threatening to spill out.

She felt him staring at her but, instead of judging her, he moved closer and put his arm around her shoulder. His voice was tender as he comforted her.

"I know that you know this, Christy, but had you been with Dawn, you might both be missing and no one would be here to look for you."

Yes, she'd heard that logic before and had even tried to convince herself of it, but logic had no place in her guilt.

Regardless, she wasn't going to allow that to stop her. She wiped away a tear that fell then choked back the rest. She glanced at her watch. "It's still early. Let's go by the Basses' store and see if they can shed some light on the night in question."

She was sad to have him pull his arm away. His compassion toward her at a weak moment only showed her initial impression of him was right. He was one of the good guys.

They climbed into Mike's SUV and headed back to the small convenience store on Mercy Highway. The store was now open for business but it wasn't busy so John agreed to step away to speak with them. His daughter, Judith, was working behind the deli counter while his son, Conner, stocked shelves in between customers.

After introducing Christy and explaining about reopening the case, Mike asked John Bass if he recalled seeing Dawn. He stared at her picture then shook his head. "I remember the case because she went to high school with my daughter, but I don't recall seeing her that night."

"Would you have been working or your son?" Christy asked.

"No. Conner joined the business ten years ago. Before that, he was still in school in Austin, so I would have been the one working at the time. I remember when this happened my daughter asked me about it. I hadn't seen anything that night."

"Thanks for your help," Mike said, shaking his hand.

Christy briefly spoke with both Judith and Conner, but it was obvious this family knew nothing. Whatever had happened to Dawn that night, she hadn't come to this store for help.

She was disappointed but at least now they could mark one thing off their list.

They climbed into Mike's SUV and headed back to the sheriff's office to get her car. That interview with the Caffertys had taken a lot out of her and had hit her harder than she'd expected. She needed time to get her thoughts together again.

Only, the emotional toll lingered as she made her way to her hotel. She took solace in her room though she couldn't stop thinking of how tightly Mrs. Cafferty had hugged her or of the hope she'd seen in both parents' eyes. She'd been searching for answers purely for her own reasons but now she wanted to find those answers and wipe away the grief for the Caffertys too.

She needed to work off some of this anxiety. Being in this town was surreal. She'd been here once during the search for Dawn twelve years ago, but Mercy was the last place she wanted to be. She'd avoided this town at all costs, which was funny since, if she'd only come with Dawn in the first place twelve years ago, as she'd promised to do, none of this would be happening.

That was all she could take. She needed to get out of this room.

She laced up her running shoes, grabbed her phone and earbuds then headed down to her car. She'd noticed the park just up the road and was looking forward to stretching her muscles and working out some angst over being back in this town and all the guilt she'd brought with her.

She drove to the park then got out and stretched. She had a lot on her mind. This was her one shot with this case and, if she blew it, she might never discover what had happened to her friend. She'd waited and trained for this all of her career. Everything was on the line.

Mike was a distraction. A very handsome distraction. She smiled, recalling the feel of his hand on her arm and her shoulder. She liked him, but nothing could ever happen between them. Besides, he was already digging in his heels about his cousin's innocence. She hoped that wouldn't deter him from keeping an open mind and investigating. Of course, she'd wanted to talk to him since he was the last person to see Dawn alive, but she'd been surprised to learn that he'd been looking into the file ever since. He'd been the one to keep it alive all of these years, even to the point that Sheriff Thompson had proclaimed this the last chance for the case.

She put in her earbuds then turned on the music as she ran, doing her best to calm her mind. The break-in at her hotel had shaken her more than she'd wanted to admit. She didn't care for small towns where everyone knew everything about your life. Dawn had told her all about Mercy and the lack of privacy. She'd felt the eyes on her since the moment she'd arrived in town but had chalked it up to being FBI. Now she wondered if anyone even cared about that. She was a stranger. That was all that mattered.

By the time the streetlights came on, she'd barely noticed the sky had darkened. That should have been her sign to end her run. She'd already been around the track several times but the rush from the exertion had kicked in and her wheels were spinning about the case. She knew the direction she wanted to go. She'd pieced together a plan in her mind about who they should interview next and what questions she wanted answers to.

Cliff Tyner was her main interview goal. She couldn't wait to call him into an interrogation room and get the answers she'd waited so long for, though she had a lot of work to do prior to that. She had to have all her ducks in a row before confronting him, but he was going to tell her what she wanted to know one way or another. He was going to tell her where her friend was buried.

She slowed to catch her breath, realizing how ominous the sky had become. The lights along the path were still flickering as they came to life. She pulled out her earbuds and shut off the music as an uncomfortable feeling swept over her. The hair on the back of her neck was standing on end. She glanced around. The trail was empty yet she felt someone watching her.

It was time to go.

She cut across the path and back to her car. Suddenly, she heard footsteps behind her. She spun around and someone tackled her, knocking her to the ground. When she tried to look up, something big and heavy came down on her head.

FIVE

Christy raised her arms to block it but only deflected the blow somewhat. Pain riddled through her as the object grazed the side of her head and she cried out. But she wouldn't let this man get the better of her.

She acted on instinct, kicking him, aiming for his kneecap. He cried out in pain and dropped the bat in his hands. The aluminum clanked against the concrete as she kicked at him again, this time sweeping his legs from under him. She fell back on her training. She'd left her gun at the hotel, so she had to rely on her hand-to-hand combat training.

She grabbed for the bat he'd dropped then swung it at the man's back.

He ran, limping into the distance, and then she heard a vehicle speeding away.

A woman ran over to her. "Are you okay? I dialed 9-1-1 when I saw that man attack you."

Her head ached but, otherwise, she wasn't hurt. "I—I think I'm okay."

"You're bleeding."

Christy reached up to her head and felt something wet and sticky. She brought down her hand and saw blood. She peeled off her jacket and pressed a piece of it to her forehead.

"It doesn't look deep but, you know, head wounds bleed like crazy," the woman said.

She saw the lights of a police cruiser and spotted Mike hopping out of his SUV behind it. He ran to her. "Christy, what happened?"

"A man attacked her with a baseball bat," the woman explained. "I saw the whole thing."

Mike turned to the patrol deputy. "Call for an ambulance."

"No, I'm fine," Christy insisted.

"You don't look fine and you might need stitches." He turned to the deputy. "Call them just in case."

"Are you okay?" he asked her and she saw concern in his eyes. She liked his compassion. They could argue about the case, but that didn't change how he treated her. He was always looking out for her.

"I'm okay," she assured him. "I didn't really get a look at him, Mike. His back was to me. I was running and he came up and grabbed me and tried to knock me out."

He looked up at the woman who'd come to her aid. "What about you? Did you recognize him?"

She bit her lip then shrugged. "No, sorry. It was dark, so I couldn't see his face. He was holding the bat however. Maybe it has his prints on it."

Mike nodded. "Let's hope so. Did either of you notice if he was wearing gloves?"

Christy glanced at her new friend, who shook her head. "I'm not sure."

"Me either," she told him.

She turned back to the woman. "Thank you. I don't know what I would have done if you hadn't come along when you did."

She smiled. "You didn't look like you needed any help, honey. You turned the tables on that fella pretty quick."

"What do you mean by that?" Mike asked her.

"Only that that guy tried to attack her. Instead, she kicked him in the knees then used the bat to fight back. He took off but he was hurt. I could tell."

He flashed Christy an impressed smile and she felt her face warm, embarrassed by the implied compliment. She'd only acted on instinct to protect herself.

The ambulance arrived and the paramedic bandaged the gash on her forehead while Mike collected the bat for evidence to try to lift prints. He took the woman's—her name was Marsha Littlefield, Christy had learned—statement then placed a call to the sheriff's office.

Christy declined to go to the hospital and instead was ready to return to the safety and comfort of her hotel room…until she remembered the break-in. Then it didn't seem so comforting to her any longer.

Still, she wasn't going to be run out of town, if that's what the attacker had had in mind. She wasn't going anywhere until she finished her investigation and discovered what had happened to her friend.

"Do you want me to drive you back to your hotel?" Mike asked her.

"No, I have my car."

"I'll follow you, then, to make sure you make it."

He remained beside her as she walked to her car and she appreciated that. She was a little woozy but it was less than a mile to her hotel and she was certain she would be fine. She wasn't even sure whether the bat had hit her or if she'd hit her head on the pavement, but it didn't matter. The wound was minor and she wouldn't let it stop her.

Mike opened her car door for her but she didn't get inside right away. She turned to him, staring up into his kind green eyes and resisting the urge to fall into his embrace. It would feel so nice to be in his arms.

She pushed away that thought. "Thanks for coming so quickly, Mike."

He smiled as his cheeks reddened. "Of course. We'll figure out who did this and why, Christy."

"We know why, don't we? Someone doesn't want this case reopened." The assailant hadn't tried to grab her phone or search her for money. Plus, he hadn't tried to harm Marsha when she'd rushed over to help.

This had been personal.

She saw the truth settle in his expression. He knew it too. She was a target because of her investigation. But, if they were trying to stop her from digging into this case, they were going to fail. She was in town to do a job and she wasn't leaving until it was complete.

She climbed into her car then made the short drive back to her hotel. Mike's SUV followed behind her and then he hopped out to walk her inside.

She liked how concerned he was with her safety. It didn't matter that they were at odds over the investigation. He was just a good guy like that and she appreciated that about him.

"You should have gone to the hospital," he told her as he used her keycard to open her door and held it while she stepped inside.

"I don't need a hospital, but I do appreciate the concern about my safety."

"Are you kidding me? Of course, I'm concerned. This is my town and you're being targeted."

She lowered herself into a chair. She was feeling a little dizzy and her head was aching, but a hot shower and some painkillers would help that. For now, all she wanted was to be alone.

"I've got patrols searching for any cameras that might have captured the attack from a neighboring business. And, hopefully, prints will come back on the bat. Maybe by tomorrow morning, we'll have some answers."

"I hope you're right."

"I should let you get some rest." He turned and walked to the door but stopped. With his hand still on the handle, he turned back to her.

"I'm sorry about this, Christy. Mercy is better than this."

Too bad she couldn't share his opinion of his hometown. So far, she'd had nothing but bad experiences here. It wasn't the first time she'd felt unwelcome in a small town either. Often, on cases with the FBI, she and her co-agents had felt a hostility even if they'd been invited into town. Many small towns didn't like outsiders, no matter what, and even though the FBI was there to help, often local law enforcement officers felt threatened by their presence too.

It wasn't so hard to block out all that negativity when she had a partner or a team with her but, here in Mercy, she was all alone. An outsider trying to bring down one of their own.

She locked the door behind him then kicked off her running shoes and changed into sweats and a T-shirt, her muscles aching with every move. By the time she returned to her cell phone, she noticed a missed call from Charlie Summers.

Her pulse sped up. Hopefully, he had something for her that would finally break this case. She hit the redial on her phone and held her breath until he picked up.

"Summers," he answered.

"Charlie, it's Christy. I saw you called. Sorry I missed you."

"Hey, Christy. No problem."

"I hope you're calling with good news about the files I asked you to look at."

"Actually, I do have something for you. I rescanned all the data the cell phone companies provided and discovered a messaging app your victim downloaded a few weeks before she vanished."

That was new. Christy and Dawn had generally kept in touch through regular or iMessage texting when they weren't together and Christy wasn't aware of any other messaging apps Dawn had been using. Also, the initial scan of the cell phone data hadn't mentioned this.

"She downloaded an app called Let's Chat. I rechecked the cell phone records for the cloned phone belonging to Cliff Tyner and his phone had the same app."

"They were chatting through the Let's Chat app?"

"They were. I counted at least a dozen messages from the day Dawn went missing, beginning at six that day. The last message he sent to her was at nine fourteen that night."

She knew from the case file reports that Mike

had pulled Christy over just after 10:00 p.m. Had she and Cliff made plans to meet up that night through the app? Had she been on her way to see him?

"Do we have access to those messages?"

"Only his messages because his phone was seized at the time of her disappearance and a copy of it was made. We were able to recover even deleted files."

"Had he deleted those messages?"

"Yes, he had. In fact, he deleted the app entirely, probably thinking that would prevent anyone from seeing them. However, you and I both know nothing is ever truly deleted."

She'd worked on plenty of cases where suspects had tried to wipe their phones clean to delete evidence, but people like Charlie could almost always recover those files. And any FBI technology was going to surpass a local sheriff's office's. She was glad to have Charlie working on this case with her.

"I'm emailing you copies of his messages to her and, based on them, you'll want to subpoena hers."

She thanked him then started to hang up.

"Hold on," he told her. "I'm not finished yet. I'm also sending you updated GPS coordinates from his cell phone. I ran them through a new mapping program to recover his GPS data from that night. You'll find it interesting too."

Now she was excited. From Charlie's statements, these messages and GPS coordinates might solve this case. "Thank you, Charlie. I'll look these over and let you know if we need anything else."

"Always happy to do my part," he said before ending the call.

She grabbed her laptop, opened it then clicked on the email she'd just received from Charlie. Screenshots of Cliff's Let's Chat messages popped up on the screen.

Why are you ignoring me, Dawn?

You can't end it this way!

Let's talk. Meet me before you go home.

What time?

I'll meet you there.

She clicked through several pages of one-sided conversations and could see the tone of the messages growing more and more intense. Something had happened between them that had obviously upset Cliff, which seemed to fit with what she knew about Dawn planning to break up with him. It seemed she'd tried and he'd been insistent upon meeting with her to try to change her mind.

Tears formed in Christy's eyes and she discreetly wiped them away. Dawn had been her friend. She'd told Christy she was breaking up with Cliff, but Christy had heard her say that before, too, then she'd chickened out and couldn't bring herself to do it. Her friend had been stuck between the freedom she enjoyed at college and her feelings for Mercy and Cliff Tyner. Christy had encouraged her to end the relationship and leave Mercy behind once and for all. Now she wondered if that advice, along with the fact that she hadn't joined Dawn for the trip as she'd planned, had placed her life in danger.

She should have been there for Dawn but she'd prioritized a trip with a boy she'd liked over her friend.

She found Mike's number but her finger hovered over his name. This didn't seem like it was going to be good news for him and would seriously ding his loyalty to his cousin. Besides, her ears were still ringing and she was certain she would want to confront Cliff right after seeing these. She wasn't up for that. She needed to rest and leave this new evidence until the morning.

But she couldn't bring herself to wait.

She felt bad for him but this was a major break for the case and for her quest to find justice for Dawn.

After he'd left Christy at the hotel, Mike dropped the bat off for processing at the lab then written up a report about the incident before calling it a night. He stopped by a local restaurant to pick up takeout. He didn't feel much like cooking, not after the call he'd gotten about Christy being attacked.

That wasn't his town. Sure, crime could happen anywhere but this was the second time Christy had been targeted since coming to Mercy. It embarrassed him to think how this made his town look.

He placed his order then sat down to wait, glancing around at tables of families already eating. He knew most of the people in this building; normal, happy families going about their lives.

He pulled out his cell phone and turned away from the families. He hadn't planned to still be single at thirty-three yet here he was. He'd dated but no relationship had grown into the future family he longed for. And watching Cliff mess up the perfect life he'd somehow been fortunate enough to fall into wasn't easy either. Envy had become a thorn in his side, a gnawing discontentment with the life and town that he loved.

Mike tried to be thankful for all he had. He loved his family and loved his job, but something had been missing from his life for a long time and he was still waiting on God to provide the solution for it.

His mind went to Christy and he couldn't stop a smile. He quickly cleared his throat and got hold of himself. Yes, she was attractive and he admired her strength and determination, but she was way out of his league. And besides, she would never forgive him for his role in Dawn's disappearance.

His phone rang. He glanced down at the number and smiled again. Christy.

He listened to her and his smile faded away as she asked him to return. He promised to head over right away. She'd sounded so serious that it made his jaw clench. Whatever she had couldn't be good.

She was all business when he knocked on her hotel room door. She opened it and showed him inside. She had her laptop set up on the dresser and a chair pulled up to it.

"What's up?' he asked her.

She looked tense. "My former FBI colleague I told you about, Charlie Summers? I finally heard back from him." She stared at him then pointed to the edge of the bed. "You should sit, Mike."

Alerts were going off in his head. This wasn't going to be good. He sat on the edge of the mattress and braced himself for whatever it was her friend had uncovered.

"Charlie was able to locate a messaging app among Cliff's phone records called Let's Chat. He also confirmed that he and Dawn were sending messages back and forth the night she disappeared. He was able to recover Cliff's messages to her but we'll have to subpoena hers since her cell phone was never recovered."

"Have you looked at them yet?" he asked.

"I did."

The look on her face told him all he needed to know. He wasn't going to like what she was about to show him.

She settled in the chair pulled up to the dresser and hit a button on the laptop, bringing up screenshots of messages between Cliff and Dawn.

What he saw sickened him. Proof that his

loyalty to his cousin all these years had been misplaced. Cliff had lied to him, had lied to everyone about the night Dawn had gone missing.

Christy ended the screenshots once they'd scrolled through all the messages. "I'll start the paperwork to subpoena Dawn's messages first thing tomorrow morning."

Mike struggled to find his voice. Seeing his cousin's lies had him stunned and questioning everything he'd believed.

He stood and looked at Christy. She'd just upended his life, but it wasn't gloating he saw in her eyes. It was empathy for him.

"Mike, I'm sorry it came to this."

He held up his hand to stop her. "You don't owe me an apology, Christy. In fact, I owe you one. You saw what I couldn't. You found truth when I refused to see it."

He headed for the door but she reached for his arm. "Where are you going?"

"To find Cliff and bring him in." Her touch was heavy on his arm and he sensed she wanted to do something to ease his pain, but there was nothing she could do to change the facts.

"Do you want me to come with you?"

He shook his head. "I need to do this on my own."

Leaving the hotel, he headed straight for his

cousin's house, bracing himself for an ugly confrontation, but bringing in Cliff for questioning was something he had to do. This new evidence was incriminating, especially when combined with the witness statement of Tony Freely. These messages corroborated what he'd said. Christy had had her sights on Cliff and now it looked like maybe she'd had a right to be focused on him. Mike had convinced himself that Freely's word couldn't be trusted but this new evidence couldn't be ignored either.

He walked up to the house and knocked. Mike heard the laughter of his nieces floating from inside and cringed. He didn't want to have to do this in front of them.

Rebecca opened the door and she was smiling, something he hadn't seen her do in a while. "Mike, hi, come on inside." Her face fell when he didn't return her happy greeting. "Is something wrong?"

"I need to speak with Cliff. It's important."

She opened the door more. He scanned the room and saw Cliff and the girls at the dining room table finishing up dinner. They looked to be a normal happy family tonight. He knew that didn't happen often and he hated to disrupt a good night for Rebecca and the girls.

But he had a job to do.

Cliff looked at him and tensed. "What's up, Mike?"

He turned to Rebecca. "I'd rather not do this with the girls in the room. Can you take them out?"

She glanced at Cliff then shrugged and gathered the girls. "Let's go to the bedroom and let Daddy and Uncle Mike talk."

The girls fussed about having to leave but she shooed them out of the room.

Cliff stood to face him. "Has something happened?"

"Yeah, it has. I need you to come down to the sheriff's office and answer some questions."

"What's this about, Mike?"

"You know exactly what this is about. There's new information in the Dawn Cafferty case that has brought up some questions I need you to answer."

His face lost color but he grabbed his jacket and keys. He walked to Rebecca, who had come back into the room, and was standing at the base of the hallway. "Everything is going to be okay. I'll be back in a while."

He exited but Mike remained. He glanced at the table and saw evidence of supper dishes and uneaten food. It was already after 10:00 p.m. and he knew the girls had school in the morning. "It's kind of late for supper, isn't it?" he asked Rebecca.

Her face reddened and she folded her arms. "We take what we can get, Mike."

"A woman was attacked earlier this evening at the walking trail. It's possible Cliff was involved. How long has he been home, Rebecca?"

She shrugged. "A couple of hours."

Long enough to have attacked Christy at the walking trail then make it home for a nice supper with his family. "Are you sure?"

She wouldn't look him in the eyes or give him a specific time, and he knew why. She didn't want to be the one to offer proof that her husband had been involved in assaulting Christy. She was trying to protect him, just as everyone in the family had done for the past twelve years, believing Cliff was a victim of false accusations.

Now Mike knew those allegations were true.

He walked outside. Cliff was already sitting in the passenger's seat of Mike's SUV, so he slid in behind the wheel and started the engine.

"Mike, tell me what's going on."

There was so much that Mike wanted to ask him but he needed to wait until they were at the office in the interrogation room. He couldn't give Cliff knowledge of what they'd uncovered beforehand. "You'll find out once we get to the SO."

They made it there and Mike led him to the interrogation room. He sensed the tension in Cliff. He should be worried.

He walked into the conference room where Christy was waiting. He'd texted her on the way to Cliff's and told her he was bringing him in. "He's here," Mike told her.

She nodded then grabbed her files and headed for the interrogation room. She'd changed into a suit and cleaned up after her encounter. Except for the bruises he knew were now covered by her sleeves and the bandage on her forehead, no one would have known what she'd been through in the past few hours. It amazed him how she could go from bruised and battered to calm and in charge in a matter of minutes.

He followed behind her as they entered the room where Cliff was waiting. She'd been wanting the chance to question Cliff herself and Mike wasn't sure he would be able to get through an interrogation without his emotions overwhelming him.

"Mr. Tyner, I'm special agent Christy Williams of the FBI. I'm in town to reopen the Dawn Cafferty missing persons case."

Cliff immediately went on the defense. "I

don't know what this has to do with me. I had nothing to do with Dawn's disappearance. I keep saying it and it doesn't change."

She sat down, but Mike preferred to lean against the wall, his arms folded as he did his best to hide his anger and disappointment at this new information and what it meant for his cousin. He'd spent the past twelve years trying to find something to move this case along and, now that they had new evidence, it didn't make him feel better. Because it was more than just proof of his involvement in Dawn's disappearance and possible murder—it was also proof that Cliff had been lying to him all these years.

Christy didn't waste time listening to his excuses. "I'd like to go back with you over the night that Dawn vanished. You and she were dating at the time, correct?"

"Yes. We'd been dating on and off for three years."

"Did you speak with her that day? Did you know she was coming back into town?"

"We talked on the phone the day before and she said she was driving home in two days."

"And did you have any contact with her on the day she vanished?"

"No."

Mike noticed the questioning look on Christy's face. "No contact at all?"

She was handing Cliff all the rope he needed to hang himself. "The police took my phone and copied it, so you know I didn't call or text her that day at all."

She smiled at his attempt to misdirect her. He was right that there was no evidence they'd texted or spoken on the phone, but the records proved they'd had contact. "So you didn't make any plans to meet up with her?"

"No."

Anger burned through Mike. If he didn't know better, he would believe his cousin's story. He had believed his story and, even now, he didn't detect a hint of deception. Only, he did know better. He knew what was coming and Cliff should have known too.

Christy pulled out photos of the Let's Chat messages and Mike saw Cliff visibly wither.

"Our tech experts at the FBI were able to recover a messaging app called Let's Chat from the data from your cell phone. These are the messages you sent to Dawn on the day she vanished." She read through them one by one. "As you can see, the tone of your messages gets more and more aggressive and you did make arrangements to meet up with her before she went home."

Cliff's face paled and he stumbled to reply. "I didn't—I mean we didn't—"

"Didn't what?" Her face and tone warned him not to lie to her again.

Cliff rubbed his hand through his hair. "We did make plans to meet up but she never showed. I waited for over an hour before I realized she wasn't coming, so I went home."

"You didn't call her to find out what was keeping her?"

He shook his head. "No, I didn't call her. I didn't message her. I figured she just didn't want to see me. I figured that was it. It was over. So I just went home. I didn't know something had happened to her until the next day."

"So you deleted the app and all its information."

"People were already giving me funny looks and whispering around me. I knew everyone thought I'd done something to her. I knew I would be a suspect."

Mike slammed his hand down on the table in front of his cousin. "So you lied! You were more worried about yourself than about finding the woman you supposedly loved."

Cliff stared up at him then crumbled. "I'm

not proud of myself, Mike. I panicked. But I was right. I was the first person the sheriff's office came looking at. They suspected me of hurting her and I didn't."

Mike shook his head. "You lied to everyone, Cliff, and lying to the police only serves to strengthen the case against you."

"But I didn't do it. I didn't hurt Dawn. I didn't even see her that night."

"You've already lied to my face, Cliff. Why should I or anyone else believe you now?"

"Because I didn't see Dawn that night. Okay, so maybe I did arrange to meet with her, but she never showed up. All those messages prove is that we made plans to meet up. They don't prove I saw her or did anything to her."

Mike turned away as Christy took over the interview again to hammer the final nail in Cliff's lies. "Except that we have an eyewitness who saw you with her on the side of Mercy Highway the night she vanished. This witness saw the two of you arguing and you pushing her into your truck. That gives us more than enough evidence to charge you with her murder."

His eyes widened at the possibility that he was about to be arrested.

"Why don't you come clean right now, Cliff?

Tell us what happened and what you did with her body. We know you saw her. We know the two of you fought. Did you lose your temper? Was there an accident?" Her tone softened as she looked at him. "You've lived with this for so long. Now's the time to finally tell the truth about that night."

Mike was surprised at how calm she seemed. This had been her friend yet she sounded like she wanted to help the man who'd murdered her. She sounded like an ally.

Only, Cliff wasn't ready to acquiesce. He leaned back in his chair and clammed up. "I'm not saying another word without a lawyer."

She stared at him for several moments before she grabbed her files and walked out of the room. Mike followed behind her as they put some distance between themselves and the interrogation room.

"That was intense," Mike said and she nodded. "I thought he was going to confess there for a minute."

"I think he wanted to," Christy said. "I feel like he's close."

"You were right when you said this has been following him around all these years. He's been the subject of accusations and trial by rumors since it happened. It's worn him down. He turned to drinking to try to get through it but that only made his life worse."

"I was serious when I said we had enough to charge him. Between the messages, the conflicting stories and our new eyewitness, we have enough."

"You're not going to wait for Dawn's messages?"

"No, that could take a while. Go ahead and arrest him. We'll arrange for a lineup with Freely tomorrow morning." She reached for her briefcase and stuffed the files into it. "I'm exhausted. I'm going back to my hotel to rest."

He couldn't blame her. She'd had a long day since the attack. "Do you want me to drive you?"

"No, but thanks. I'll be fine." She started to walk away but stopped at the conference room door and placed her hand on his arm. "I'm really sorry, Mike."

She walked out and he watched her go. There was no look of satisfaction on her face or in her demeanor. It was a win finally solving her friend's murder but she didn't look happy about it. He wasn't happy, either, that he'd been so deceived all of these years. All the guilt that he'd carried with him while his cousin had hidden his actions and allowed Mike to publicly defend him.

Christy could have gloated about being right but she hadn't and he appreciated that.

He watched her get into her car then headed back to the interrogation room to arrest his cousin for the murder of Dawn Cafferty.

Christy was exhausted. She didn't know if she was going to even make it to her hotel without falling asleep at the wheel. It had taken everything she'd had left in her to confront Cliff Tyner, but she'd made it.

There wasn't the sense of satisfaction in confronting Cliff Tyner that she'd expected. Where was the joy and happiness at finally finding justice for Dawn? Why wasn't it there?

Maybe it was because of the toll she'd seen such a victory had had on Mike. It had made her realize that there were no winners in this situation. Her friend was still dead and another family and community had been devastated.

Cliff Tyner would pay for his crimes and, hopefully, in the process, lead them to where he'd buried Dawn's body.

Her cell phone rang and she glanced at the screen in the cradle on the dashboard. Mike. She hit the answer button.

"Hi, Mike. How'd it go?"

"He's been booked and locked up."

"Did he say anything else?"

"No. He just glared at me the entire time as if this was all my fault."

That was a low blow. Mike had been one of the few she'd seen who had been on Cliff's side. "He was the one who lied. You have nothing to feel guilty about."

"I know. I'm just so angry at him right now and I'm too hyped up to sleep. What do you say I grab some takeout and meet you back at your hotel? We can get started on putting this case together for the prosecutor's office."

She had planned to get right to bed but it sounded like he needed someone to talk to and spending some time with Mike intrigued her. Maybe now that Cliff had been arrested and the case was solved, getting to know Mike better was a possibility. "That sounds nice."

"Great. I'll see you in about an hour?"

She was about to respond yes when bright lights from a vehicle roared up on her car and blinded her. She cried out as it hurt her eyes.

"Christy? Are you okay?"

"Yes, just someone's headlights on bright making it difficult for me to see."

She'd just assured him she was fine when

the vehicle sped up and rammed the back of her car. "Mike!" she screamed. She turned the steering wheel, fighting hard to keep her car on the road. "Someone's trying to push me off the road."

"Hold on, Christy. I'm on my way."

She'd been trained in defensive maneuvers but her little rental car was no match for the oversized pickup. She tried to see into the cab but the lights were glaring and she couldn't make out any faces. The truck rammed her again and, this time, she couldn't control it. Her car sped off the road and crossed the shoulder. She screamed as it slammed to a stop as the front end plowed into a tree. Her vision went hazy as darkness pulled her under.

SIX

Her head was spinning when the darkness faded. Sounds slowly drifted into her consciousness. The horn permanently blowing, something from the engine hissing and the panicked voice of someone calling her name.

"Christy! Christy, can you hear me? Are you hurt?"

She attempted to move and pain radiated through her from all parts of her body. She groaned and Mike must have heard it because he started calling her name again.

"Christy, can you hear me? Can you speak to me?"

"I'm…okay," she said, straining to even get the words out as the full weight of what had happened pulsed through her.

She focused her eyes and saw a large oak incredibly close to her. The front end of her car had smashed into it at a high speed and now the engine was very nearly in her lap. The front end had buckled, the seat belt had locked and the airbags had deployed, probably saving her life. However, the impact had hit her hard and now every inch of her bristled with pain. She grabbed for her neck where the pain seemed to be the worst.

"I'm nearly to you," Mike told her through the phone. "Hold on. Are you injured?"

"I'm not sure yet, but I don't think so."

Something caught her eye that brought her completely back to her senses. The truck that had run her off the road was idling nearby. Waiting, watching.

"They're still here." It seemed odd that the truck hadn't fled. Probably wanted to make sure she hadn't survived. Too bad for them.

"What? Who?"

"The truck that ran me off the road. It's still here. It's just sitting there."

She had a brief panic in wondering what they would do to her if she stumbled out of the car. It was obvious from the way they'd smashed into her that the driver hadn't planned on leaving her alive.

"Stay put. I'm on my way to you."

"Mike, please hurry," she told him.

But she wasn't just sitting and waiting for Mike to arrive to save her. She needed her gun.

She painfully turned her head to find her purse. She'd placed it on the seat beside her but it had flown off in the wreck and scattered her belongings over the floorboard. She needed to find her gun in case these assailants decided not to wait to see if she'd survived.

She unbuckled her seat belt then leaned over the console. It hurt but she pushed through it. Better a little pain now than dead later.

Christy jostled through the makeup and notecards, all the stuff that had spilled out from her purse, but her gun wasn't there. She shoved her hand under the seat and felt the cold grip of her weapon and a warm sense of satisfaction filled her. If these men wanted a fight, they would get it.

She'd hadn't been able to see how many people had been inside the truck. She couldn't take on two, especially in her slow, aching way, but she would take out at least one of them if Mike didn't get here soon.

Footsteps headed her way. She hadn't seen the flashing lights that would indicate Mike had arrived. She turned over as the footsteps approached the car.

She held her weapon doing her best to keep her hands from shaking. She wouldn't be able to get away soon enough but she could at least protect herself. She held her gun up and waited for a figure to arrive in front of the window.

A shadow from the truck's headlights silhouetted him as he approached. A gun was clearly outlined in his hand. That was enough confirmation for her. She fired at the shadow and heard the attacker cry out before he turned and ran away from the car.

Christy scrambled to right herself enough so she could see him but only managed to view him briefly as he hopped back into his pickup and sped away. Moments after he did, lights and sirens ripped through the darkness and Mike's SUV stopped in the road.

He jumped out and ran down the embankment toward her. "Christy, are you okay?"

"I shot him," she said, doing her best to hold back the tears that were threatening to shake through her. "He had a gun and I shot him then he took off."

He glanced to where she indicated then turned back to her. "I called an ambulance. It'll be here soon."

"You should go after him."

"No. Making sure you're okay has to be my top priority. Did you see his face? Can you identify him?"

"No, but he was driving a dark truck like the

one Cliff has. It should have some damage on the side of it where he ran into me."

He didn't ask her any more questions but stayed with her until the ambulance arrived then helped her to it as two paramedics started looking her over.

"He tried to kill me, Mike."

He put his arm around her and held her and she was glad for the comfort.

"I know."

She was beginning to think clearly now. The only reason she would be in danger in this town was her investigation. "Someone doesn't want me to solve this case." She locked eyes with him and saw he was thinking the same thing. Her only known enemy was the man she was hunting who'd murdered her friend.

"It couldn't have been Cliff. He was sitting in a jail cell. I placed him there myself."

That realization hit her hard. She'd been so sure that Cliff had to be the killer but why else would someone want to harm her?

Was it possible she'd charged a truly innocent man of murder?

Mike stared at the totaled car. Christy very easily could have been killed by the impact of that tree, which was likely what whomever had run her off the road had intended. The front end was crushed like an accordion but the seat belt and airbag had kept her from serious injury.

He glanced at her still in the ambulance. She didn't appear to have any broken bones. The smell of crunched metal and engine fluids was strong and shattered glass lay on the ground. But he also spotted something else by the driver's-side door mixed in with the broken glass and dirt. He knelt and glanced at the splotch of red.

Blood. She had hit him when she'd fired.

He walked to his car and pulled out his kit to collect the blood. If they could use it to get a DNA sample and that person was in the system, it would make solving this hit-and-run easier. Of course, that would also take time and there were other investigative measures he would pursue as well. For now, the only person he didn't suspect—couldn't suspect—was his cousin. Despite that he couldn't rule Cliff out from the other events, there was no way he was involved in this attack on Christy. He'd been at the jail ever since Mike had picked him up. Yet Christy had mentioned seeing a pickup truck like the one Cliff owned.

He pulled out his cell phone and dialed the

sheriff's office. Deputy Drake Shaw answered and Mike gave him a quick rundown of what had happened. "Do me a favor and check the jail. Make sure he's still there."

Drake agreed and Mike waited until he got back on the phone. "He's sitting in the jail cell, Mike. I'm looking right at him."

That was a relief, but it also added more questions. "Thanks for making sure."

He ended the call and knew he had to do more. Just to be certain, he would do his due diligence and drive by the house to make sure someone hadn't used Cliff's pickup to try to implicate him in this wreck.

John Rapport, one of the paramedics, approached him with an update. "There doesn't appear to be any major injuries. She's conscious and alert but she admits to losing consciousness momentarily, so we've recommended she go to the ER for a CT scan."

"Great. Tell her I'll meet her there to drive her back to her hotel in a bit. I need to secure this scene then check something out first."

John nodded and hurried back up to the waiting ambulance.

The first deputies arrived and Mike left the scene in the hands of Deputy Warren to oversee, even handing over the blood evidence for him to send to forensics to process. They would also need to take samples of the side of her vehicle to match to the offending vehicle, if and when it was located, to tie that vehicle to this incident.

Mike grabbed Christy's briefcase and laptop from the back seat. She might need those later on so it was best to get them now before the car was towed. He climbed into his SUV then drove toward his cousin's house and got out. Cliff's pickup was still parked in the driveway right where it had been when Mike had picked him up earlier that evening. Mike got out and walked to the side. He saw no indication of any scratches or dents to indicate Cliff's truck had been involved in Christy's attack.

His muscles relaxed a bit at that knowledge even though he knew Cliff couldn't have driven it. He was glad to know it was another vehicle entirely involved.

The front door opened and Rebecca hurried out when she saw him. "What are you doing here, Mike? Cliff called and told me what you did. You arrested him." Her tone was full of shock and accusation.

"I had no choice. I have to go where the evidence takes us. But that's not why I'm here.

Has Cliff's truck been here all day? Did you let anyone borrow it?"

She shook her head. "No. It's been sitting right there since you two left. No one has bothered it. Cliff has the keys."

He touched the hood and noted it was cold. Good. No one had used it to run cover for Cliff or to try to frame him for their actions. That meant there was another pickup out there that matched his.

That wasn't so unusual. Cliff's truck didn't stand out as unique in any aspect. It was a standard make and model and a popular color. It also bore no vanity tags or stickers like some vehicles he'd seen. The only identifiable thing about it was the toolbox, but that wasn't unusual to see in Mercy County either.

"Cliff said he's going to have to spend the night in jail, Mike," Rebecca shrieked. "How could you do that to family?"

Her attitude irritated him a bit. It wouldn't be the first time Cliff hadn't come home at night, but she was acting as if the family would fall apart without him. Knowing how Cliff had lied to him, he didn't have a lot of sympathy toward his current predicament.

"I did my job. Cliff lied to the police about

the night Dawn vanished. He did have contact with her and he made plans to see her."

Her eyes widened and she stepped back and gasped. "You think he did it?"

"No, I don't. I just…" He trailed off. He'd lost his faith in Cliff for a while yet this new attack against Christy had made him rethink. Obviously, Cliff hadn't been involved in the attack but did that mean he also hadn't been involved in the murder?

This assault had seemed targeted, so they'd assumed it had had something to do with Dawn's case. But could it just have been an act of road rage or a targeting of an outsider who'd arrived in town? The gun and sticking around to make sure she was dead told him this was no random act of violence. That meant that, unless Christy had brought danger with her to Mercy County, there might still be a killer on the loose.

Christy was still sore but she was feeling better and glad that she hadn't been seriously injured in the car wreck. Mostly, she was angry that someone was trying to harm her and what that meant for her investigation. She'd staked her reputation that Cliff had killed Dawn but now she was questioning everything. Why else would someone in this town want to hurt her?

A knock on the door grabbed her attention. She glanced up to see Mike standing there. Relief rushed through her at seeing him walk through the door. The paramedic had given her his message that he would come and take her back to her hotel but it had been several hours and she'd figured he'd forgotten or gotten caught up with something else. She'd already had her tests run and been examined and cleared by the doctor. She'd even changed back into her street clothes from the hospital attire and had been preparing to call a cab since her vehicle was totaled. She was going to have to replace her rental car but that might take her a day or two to work through the necessary paperwork.

"How are you feeling?" he asked as he entered the room.

"I'm okay. Just really sore. If they were wanting me dead, they failed." She tried to put on a brave face and make a joke about it but it bothered her more than she wanted to let on. "Did you find out anything?"

"Well, it obviously wasn't Cliff that ran you off the road. He was still at the jail. I went by his house and checked out his truck in case someone was using it or trying to frame him. His was still sitting in his driveway and it was undamaged. I'll run DMV info to find out who has a similar make and model, but I can already tell you it will likely be a high number. Texas is known for its pickup trucks and Mercy is no exception. Cliff's truck is older but still a popular make, model and color around here."

She couldn't even process what it meant that Cliff wasn't involved in this attack against her and how it related to his culpability in Dawn's disappearance. For now, she concentrated only on the person who'd run her off the road. "We should reach out to body shops too to see if anyone with a truck matching that description brings it in."

He nodded. "I'll do that. In the meantime, the lab has the blood and paint evidence. It probably won't help us find the truck or driver but we can use it to verify a suspect once we identify him."

She was glad he was on the ball and already checking out leads. He was a good investigator and she was happy to have him on her side.

"Are you ready to be released?"

"Almost. The nurse is bringing in my discharge papers. They told me to rest. I've got some whiplash but otherwise I wasn't injured."

Of course, her aches and pains from the earlier attack at the walking trail only added to the stiffness she was feeling now. She was surprised she could even move.

He waited until the nurse entered and handed her the papers to officially discharge her then he assisted her outside to his SUV, his strong arms helping keep her steady as they walked to his vehicle. He held the door while she slid into the passenger's seat. His hand holding on to hers was meant to be protective yet she felt a tingling at his touch.

He remained close to her as they arrived at the hotel. She bobbed her head at Steve, who was working the front desk as they entered, then headed up to her room as he waved. She was glad to have Mike by her side and looking out for her, especially since she was moving slowly.

He unlocked her hotel room door then held it while she entered. Her foot caught on the carpet and she stumbled, nearly falling.

Mike's strong arms caught her. "I've got you," he said.

She clung to him as he steadied her, her heart pounding at being so close to him. She couldn't deny her attraction to him or the spark between them and, for a moment, she had no desire to. Basking in his embrace felt too good.

Her knees buckled and Mike's grip tightened against her as he helped her to a chair. "Can I get something for you?"

She was still dizzy from the adrenaline of the moment but managed to pull herself together. "Could you hand me the pain reliever from the bathroom?"

He walked into the bathroom then returned with a bottle of over-the-counter pills and a glass of water, which he handed to her. "They didn't give you anything stronger than this?"

"They did give me a prescription for something stronger but I don't want to take it unless I need to." She downed two pills then handed the glass and bottle back to him. Their fingers touched in the exchange and he smiled down at her as he set the items on the end table within reach of the bed. Maybe nothing could ever happen between them, but she was still thankful he was there.

"Do you want me to order you some food?" he offered, always thinking of her.

"No. If I get hungry, I'll order something. Right now, I think I just want to get some rest."

"I'll call and check on you in the morning to see if you want me to come by and get you or if you feel up to coming into the office."

"Definitely come get me tomorrow morning. I don't want to lose any time." She wasn't going to waste valuable time laying around no matter the pain tomorrow might bring. "If your cousin isn't the one targeting me then I want to know who is."

He shifted from foot to foot, hesitant to bring up the subject. "About that. I should ask you if there's anyone you know of who might have followed you to Mercy. An old boyfriend maybe? Or someone you investigated who has a grudge against you?"

She knew he had to ask that question—she would have, too, if the tables were turned—but her life before coming to Mercy consisted of work and home. Personal relationships had been practically nonexistent. "I don't know of anyone. Nothing happened to me before I came here. It's been over a year since I even went on a date."

"What about your cases? Could someone be holding a grudge against you because you put them away? Or any recent suspects just released from prison?"

Again, that seemed like a dead end. "Most of the cases I've worked the past few years have been with a team or local law enforcement. I can't think of any case where I would have been seen as responsible for an arrest or conviction. I'll check with my special agent in charge, but I can't imagine this is related to my work or my personal life. No, I think this threat is local and it must have to do with Dawn's case. Maybe Cliff has friends who want to try to run me out of town."

Now it was his turn to look skeptical. "That's doubtful. Cliff used to be very popular. He was a football star when he played, helping the school win multiple championships. However, over the years, as the accusations about Dawn grew, people distanced themselves from him. Once he started drinking to cope, things got worse. He's more of an outcast in the community than anything else. I doubt he has friends close enough to risk their freedom by trying to kill a federal agent."

She thought about that and realized he was right. Few people would have those kinds of friends in reality. But maybe they weren't trying to kill her but only scare her into giving up the investigation. Either way, she wanted to know for certain. "We should still check it out. I don't want to take anything for granted again."

That was how she'd wound up in this situation. She'd been so certain about Cliff and she still wasn't convinced he hadn't killed Dawn, but something else was going on.

"He hangs out at McClain's Bar. I'll talk to the staff there and see if there are any people he associates with regularly then check them out too."

"I wish I could be there tonight to help you out." She wanted answers but spending time with him was also an appealing prospect. Her heart was willing but her muscles protested the thought with a sharp spasm in her neck. She grimaced and reached to rub it.

"They'll probably be more likely to talk to me than a federal agent anyway," Mike insisted. "You get some rest. I'll see you in the morning."

She forced herself to get up and pull the locks on the door after he left to make certain no one was getting inside. She didn't like to admit that tonight's event had her shaken. She was used to hunting down criminals for victims, not being the victim, and realizing that someone wanted her to stop trying to uncover what had happened to her friend was eye-opening.

She grabbed the files from her briefcase and tried her best to focus on them but the events of the day had taken their toll.

Finally, she leaned back on the pillow and

closed her eyes, praying the pain in her neck would decrease by tomorrow, though she'd always heard the next day was even worse.

But, as she drifted to sleep, her thoughts were not on her pain as much as on the feeling of Mike's embrace.

Mike felt bad for leaving Christy alone yet there was nothing he could do for her tonight. She needed rest and time to recover and his hanging around wasn't going to help with that even though he found being around her enticing. He wasn't sure if his desire to protect her was due to his loyalty to his hometown or his growing attraction to her, but he couldn't deny it had felt good to hold her even when it had been out of necessity. She'd fit so easily into his arms and the way she'd stared up at him had set his nerve endings going. His every instinct had been to pull her closer and kiss her but her knees giving way had brought him back to his senses. She'd been injured and he'd nearly used the moment to take advantage. That wasn't right.

He didn't know if she would be physically able to work tomorrow or not, but he needed to keep going if for no other reason than to find the person who had targeted her.

He'd meant it when he'd told her that Cliff didn't have many friends in town any longer. His wife and family were pretty much everyone he had in his life. Making sure was a duty he had to follow up on.

He drove to McClain's Bar and parked. Cliff frequented this place. He was a regular here. Mike knew that because he'd been called several times to pick up his cousin after a night of heavy drinking and brawling. If anyone knew who his friends were, it would be the staff at McClain's.

He got out and walked inside. The lights were low, music was playing on the sound system and many of the seats at the bar taken. Several tables were scattered throughout the space and people were grouped there.

He walked to the counter and a female bartender greeted him with a smile. "Hi there, Deputy. I'm surprised to see you. Your cousin isn't here tonight."

"I know. I'm actually looking for information about Cliff's friends. Can you tell me who he hangs out with regularly when he's here?"

She ducked her head toward a table in the back. "He mostly sits with those two. Devon Mitchell and Jerry Paul. They're all three regulars."

"Thanks."

He headed over to the table to introduce himself. He'd seen these men before with Cliff but hadn't been aware they regularly hung out. He would run a check to make sure they didn't have criminal records or tendencies toward mischief but, for now, he just wanted a feel for whether or not one or both of them would do something to help Cliff avoid jail.

"Gentlemen, I'm Deputy Mike Tyner. Cliff's cousin."

They glanced up from their conversation and gave him the once-over.

"We know who you are," Jerry stated. "Cliff talks about you all the time."

"He does?" That surprised him. He and Cliff weren't really that close except when he was pulling him out of the bars and driving him home.

"Sure he does," Devon confirmed. "He says you're the only person in town who believes in him and doesn't think he killed that girl. If he thinks you're okay, then you're okay to us too."

Mike gritted his teeth, wondering what they would think of him if they knew he'd arrested Cliff earlier in the day for doing just that. He didn't feel too good about it. That much was certain. And to know his cousin told people that he was the only one who believed in him touched a nerve. He had spent the past twelve years trying to prove Cliff's innocence without success. Then he'd turned on him so easily at the first sign of new evidence.

New evidence that proved Cliff had spent years lying to him.

"Do you fellas have an opinion about his guilt or innocence?"

They both shook their heads.

"I know he didn't do it," Devon said.

"How do you know that?" Mike asked him.

"Because I know Cliff. He's not capable of that kind of violence."

Jerry agreed with his friend's assessment. "I used to play football with Cliff, so I knew him back then too, and even then, I never believed he killed his girlfriend. He loved her too much and the only time I saw him get violent was tackling someone on the football field."

They had to know how much his cousin drank if they were his drinking buddies. "So you've never seen him get aggressive or violent when he was drinking? Because I know from firsthand experience I've been called for a few fights he got into in this place."

Devon shrugged. "Well, he might have a hot temper but only when he's provoked. Usually, he's a stand-up guy."

"What kind of vehicles do you fellas drive?" Mike asked.

"Jeep Cherokee for me," Devon stated.

"Dodge truck," Jerry said.

The Dodge was a similar truck to Cliff's so that piqued Mike's interest. "Yeah? Can I look at it?"

He shook his head. "It's not here. I'm in my wife's car tonight. She needed to load some flowers for her garden, so we switched."

That seemed awfully convenient to Mike. "What time did you get here, Jerry?"

"Eight forty-five. Why?"

"Can anyone confirm that?"

"I can," Devon insisted. "I got here an hour before he did."

Mike jotted down notes then asked Jerry for his address.

"What's this about?" Devon demanded. "Why are you questioning us this way?"

He sighed and decided to be honest with them. "Cliff is in jail. We found new evidence that proved he lied to the police about the night his girlfriend vanished. A few hours later, Agent Williams, the FBI agent in town to work on this case, was run off the road and nearly killed. I figure either someone was trying to cover for Cliff or somebody else really killed the girl and is trying to stop this investigation. The sooner I can rule out someone covering for him, the sooner I can start looking for other suspects."

They shared a glance that seemed to imply they understood.

Mike continued. "I checked my cousin's pickup and it wasn't the one used to run Agent Williams off the road. Whoever did that will have some damage to their vehicle and, Jerry, your truck matches the description of the one she described that ran her down."

He nodded and gave Mike his address. "It should be at home now, parked in the garage. Just knock and my wife will let you see it. I'll text her to let her know you're coming by."

"Thank you. I have to ask you both if either of you or anyone you know would do something to try to steer this investigation away from Cliff?"

Devon shook his head. "Look, I like Cliff, but not enough to risk going to jail for him."

Mike glanced at Jerry, who seconded his friend's sentiment. "We're friends, but I've got my own family and my own problems to worry about."

"What about any other friends of his?"

"To my knowledge, he doesn't have any," Devon offered. "We're it."

Mike was satisfied with their statements. He thanked them both then walked back to the bartender he'd spoken to earlier. She was able to confirm the times both men had arrived and stated she hadn't seen either of them leave since arriving.

That was good. That meant neither man could have been involved in the attack against Christy and that it was unlikely that someone had targeted her to help Cliff.

Mike made a quick stopover at Jerry's house and checked out his pickup. It wasn't damaged and his wife confirmed she'd borrowed it to haul some gardening supplies. It was looking more and more certain to him that his cousin couldn't have had any involvement in the attack on Christy.

And if he hadn't been involved then who had been and why?

It was time to look elsewhere for suspects.

Christy was definitely feeling sore the next morning but she wasn't going to let the pain stop her from her investigation. She wanted answers worse than she wanted relief.

Mike arrived at her hotel room bright and early and she greeted him at the door, ready to go. A whiff of his aftershave sent her mind back to the night before and being in his arms. She pushed that memory from her mind. She needed to focus on the case, not her emotions.

As they drove to the sheriff's office, he filled her in about his interviews with Cliff's friends and the work he'd done the previous evening to make sure no one was trying to run cover for Cliff. She had to admit, he was thorough. But that meant they now had to consider that either Cliff was innocent as he claimed, had a secret accomplice no one knew about, or else someone was targeting her for another reason altogether.

Mike had a plan of action ready. "I think we should turn our focus back to my theory that her car broke down that night and someone picked her up. We interviewed every tow truck driver in the county back then and no one had a record of picking her up, but something happened to that car. Dawn didn't just go missing, so did her vehicle, and it's much harder to bury a car than a body."

Christy recalled reading through the interviews with tow truck drivers. Nothing had stood out to her, either, but it never hurt to reinterview possible witnesses. Loyalties changed over the years and someone who might have refused to speak then might open up a lead for them today. "Okay, let's do it."

"Are you sure you're up for this?" Mike asked as he saw her grimace in pain as she lowered herself into a chair in the conference room.

She was still sore from the night before but she wasn't going to let it stop her. "I might be moving slower today but I won't quit. Whoever ran me off the road last night can't get away with it. Have there been any updates besides the friends you spoke with last night?"

"The prints on the housekeeper's locker at the hotel came back. They matched guess who? Stacy Cooper. Whoever broke in and stole her card was being careful. There were no prints on the knife or the threatening note. I also can't remember Cliff ever having a knife like that."

"What about the prints on the bat from the walking trail?"

"The only good print on it belonged to you. We found one camera that picked up the attack but it was too far to really be helpful. You couldn't see the assailant's face or get any info on the vehicle he left in. All we could see was that it was a light-colored, four-door sedan."

She was disappointed but not awfully surprised. "So it's a bust then."

"I did start a search for vehicles that match the description of the one that ran you off the road. Like I said, it's a lot that came back so we'll need to go through them to eliminate them one by one."

She sighed, wondering if people really understood that a big part of performing investigations was drudging through paperwork and mundane details like that.

"Are you sure you don't recall seeing any distinguishing marks or decals on the truck?" he asked and she had to say no.

"I didn't notice any but it was dark."

"Okay then. I'll ask the sheriff about getting a few deputies to help sort through these."

"You take care of that then make up a list of names and addresses of tow truck drivers you want to interview. I need to work on the subpoena for Dawn's phone records and Let's Chat messages and get that sent." It would be a while before they would receive those files from the cellular and app companies but she hoped they might provide definitive answers once they arrived. However, they couldn't wait on them to build their case…if there even was still a case.

The problem was that she had enough evidence to convict Cliff Tyner for Dawn's murder and she was certain Dawn's Let's Chat messages would only strengthen the case against him. Only, now she was having doubts about his guilt. If the killer was behind these attacks on Christy, he'd messed up. In trying to keep her from investigating, he'd ruined his chance to have someone else take the fall for his actions. If Cliff was guilty, then she was going to have to find enough evidence to alleviate her doubts. If he wasn't, she wouldn't rest until she'd found the real culprit.

Christy opened her computer, thankful that it hadn't been damaged in the wreck and to Mike for bringing it to her. Taking hours to set up a new one was time she didn't have to spare. She opened a file and typed out the subpoena then emailed it to the sheriff to approve and forward to the court. She was ready to go conduct those interviews when Mike returned.

"Sheriff Thompson assigned two groups of patrol deputies to check on the names on that list for us," he explained. "I asked them to look for any damage to the side of the pickup or any signs of recent repairs. I've also had someone start calling around to body shops. Hopefully, we'll know something more by this afternoon."

"That's good. Are we ready to start reinterviewing the tow truck companies?"

"Yes, I made a list of six names in the area. They should be able to tell us through records if anyone picked Dawn up the night she vanished."

They'd already checked those records twelve years earlier but, as she'd said before, time changed things. People's perspectives and loyalties shifted. "Great. Let's get going."

She hoped this lead would provide the answers to their questions.

SEVEN

Mike pulled out his notebook as they left Mitchell Towing and marked through the name on his list.

"How many more do we have?" Christy asked him.

He glanced at the list he'd made. "Two more."

They'd spent most of the morning interviewing various towing companies throughout the county and even in the neighboring county. After coming up empty with new information about Dawn's case, Christy was beginning to think this lead was a dead end.

"Want to grab some lunch before we continue?" he asked her and she was thankful for the break.

"Sure." The morning had been exhausting to get through and her head and neck were killing her. She'd already downed pain relievers once. It was past time for another dose.

He drove to a diner and they took a seat at a table outside. She ordered a sandwich and chips and he ordered a burger and fries.

"I'm not sure this is moving us forward," she said, putting voice to her concerns as she dug through her purse for the pills and took two. "If there had been any record of one of these companies towing Dawn's car, then we should have heard something by now or found her car."

"That may be true but where's a better place to hide a car than among other cars?"

She could see he was hopeful this lead was going to take them somewhere, but she wasn't as confident. "I don't know, Mike. This feels like a dead end."

He put down his burger. "It's only two more companies. Let's just get through this. I know you're anxious for something to happen but this is a good lead and we should follow it completely."

She finally agreed, but he was right. This felt like a waste of time in her opinion. Unfortunately, she didn't have a more pressing lead to turn to.

She ate a few bites of her sandwich before she glanced up and caught him staring. He quickly looked away as an embarrassed smile crossed his face.

"What is it?" she asked, her own face warming at the attention.

"Nothing. I was just wondering about you. How long have you been with the FBI?" he asked her, turning the conversation to a more personal note.

She didn't mind. "Ten years. I joined right after college."

"You told Mr. and Mrs. Cafferty that you joined the FBI in order to solve this case, but there must be more to it. Were you a criminal justice major in college?"

She shook her head as she sipped her drink. The pain was beginning to subside. "Not at first. I was an English major. I was a year from graduating when Dawn went missing. We'd been roommates since freshman year and had grown to be close friends. When she went missing, I was so confused. I remember feeling so helpless and out of control. No one was talking or saying anything about her case. I mean, I guess they were, but I wasn't privy to any of that. I wanted to understand what was happening, but I really didn't understand why the police were doing what they were doing.

"I sat out the spring semester after she vanished but when I returned to school, I changed my major to criminal justice. I made it my mission to learn everything I could about investigative procedures and I dug into the case as best I could until I joined the FBI, because they gave me the best training to try to figure this out. Even then, I never felt ready to really tackle it. I spent so long being afraid to dig into this case."

He understood. "I get that. It's been in my face since she went missing, so I never had to think about worrying about whether or not to investigate. I had a personal link to it. I needed to solve it. Unfortunately, I watched it go through investigator after investigator with no success. If they made any headway, it was to blame Cliff. That was never good enough for me. Only, the longer the case lingers, the less likely it is to be solved. I know that."

"Cold cases are often solved just because of the passage of time. Loyalties change and time diminishes the urgency of people's perspectives. It's always better to solve a case before it goes cold, but that doesn't mean it's unsolvable."

"I always believed we would find her body by now. I can't believe it's still not been found."

She agreed. "I know. That's always made me wonder too. I have no doubt she's dead. I never bought into the theory that she ran away, changed her name and was out there living her life under an assumed identity. I knew her better than that."

"Well, she hasn't been living somewhere using her social security number or touched her bank accounts. Her car hasn't been registered anywhere either. I check at least once a year."

She was glad to hear he'd continued debunking that theory because she'd never bought into it. "Dawn had nothing to run from. Aside from her family, I probably knew her best. She loved being in college. She was torn between her feelings for Cliff and the desire to spread her wings and find a bigger world than she knew here in Mercy. But she loved her parents and she was looking forward to living her life. As a matter of investigative integrity, I did feel the need to make certain to document the reasons why the theory that she left on her own wasn't viable. That way, if this case ever goes to trial without a body, a defense lawyer can't use that argument. I mean I guess they can try, but I would have the proof to rebut them."

He nodded. "You're thorough. I like that."

She felt her face warm again. Why did she care so much what this deputy thought of her? She wasn't sure, but she did. And the admiration went both ways. She'd expected Deputy Mike Tyner to be someone who was lazy and hadn't done his job. Why else would this case have languished unsolved? Now she understood better the reasons. It wasn't because of Mike's lack of trying. In fact, he was the only one still keeping it alive. The more she got to know this man, she more she liked him.

She tried to push her thoughts back to the interviews. Too many times she found herself focusing on the lines of his jaw or the strength in his hands. She'd leaned on him once too often and that was a mistake. She was growing too close to Mike, dangerously close, since nothing could ever happen between them. She would be leaving town once this case was over and he was a small-town soul.

It was too bad because she realized she would have liked to get to know him better.

"Okay," she said, turning their attention back to what really mattered. The case. "Let's finish conducting those interviews. Hopefully, one of these last two places can provide some further information."

He glanced at his watch. "Both of the next places are on the other side of town. Do you mind if I stop by my cousin's house to check in on my aunt, Rebecca and the girls?"

She hesitated at the idea of facing the family of the man she'd just arrested. "Are you sure it's a good idea for me to be there? I'd feel awkward since I just had their husband and father arrested."

He chuckled. "Join the club. I think they know we're just doing our jobs. I should still check in with them regardless. Until Cliff's initial court appearance, I feel responsible for them." Yet he must have realized how uncomfortable that would be for her and offered her another option. "I can drop you off at the sheriff's office if you'd prefer but, I promise, I won't stay long."

"No, it's fine. No need to make a special trip for my sake." If need be, she could remain in the car while Mike looked in on his family. It was actually very sweet that he was worried about them, but that spoke to the goodness of his character and actually only endeared him to her more.

He headed across town and her level of uncertainty rose as he pulled into the driveway of a small house in a suburban neighborhood.

"I'll wait here," she insisted. "I can use the time to go over my notes and prepare for the other interviews."

He agreed then exited just as the school bus pulled up to the curb and two little girls got out.

"Uncle Mike, Uncle Mike," the older one

yelled then ran at him, screaming with delight at seeing him. The smaller one followed her sister. Mike picked her up and lifted her above his head then brought her down, tickling her as she fell into his arms. She squealed in laughter while the other niece reached for him yelling, "Me next! Me next, Uncle Mike!"

Christy laughed at the scene and couldn't help but be reminded of her own dreams of a husband and family one day. She'd always believed she would marry and have kids, but here she was, already in her thirties and still single. She'd had plenty of dates when she'd wanted them, though that wasn't often. She'd thrown herself into her work and learning her craft so she could solve this case one day. She'd made it her mission and had put that dream of a family life on hold. Now she realized it might never be realized.

She just couldn't get past her fear of messing up. She'd chosen a boy over her friend and look what had happened.

Nonetheless, in a moment like this, it pained her to see what she might be missing.

Mike fell to the ground and the girls hopped on him until their mother finally came to the door.

"Girls, it's time to come inside. Thank Uncle Mike for stopping by."

"Thank you!" they both said in unison.

Mike hugged them both and watched them hurry inside. Rebecca glared at him then walked back inside, too, although another woman— Christy assumed it was his aunt—exited the house and spoke to him. After a moment, she also walked back inside without inviting him in.

She watched as his shoulders slumped. She recognized a rejection when she saw it and was sad that he was being shunned by his family for doing his job. She hated her role in it, only because of Mike's sake.

He got back into the SUV and started the engine without addressing what had just occurred. "They don't need anything. Apparently, Cliff's initial appearance is later this afternoon."

She glanced at her watch. "Do we need to put off the rest of the interviews until tomorrow?"

He shook his head. "I think we have time and I'd rather go ahead and get them over with."

She could read between the lines. He didn't want to spend the next few hours brooding about the dustup with his family. She smiled at him. "Your nieces are adorable, by the way. You really enjoy playing the doting uncle, don't you?"

The mention of the girls caused a grin to

spread across his face. "Are you kidding me? They're amazing. I can't wait until I have a house full of kids myself. One of the things that really irritates me about my cousin is that he has everything I've ever wanted. The adoring wife. The beautiful kids. A place to call home. It's all I've ever wanted for myself."

She liked seeing this manly man be so wistful about wanting a family. It was too adorable.

"What about you?" he asked her. "Do you ever think about having a family?"

"I used to. When I was younger, I imagined my life very differently. I wanted to teach literature and spend my summers hanging out with my kids." She felt her face warm at how silly that sounded. "I was so young and naïve back then. I thought nothing bad ever happened in the world. Dawn's disappearance changed everything. It changed me."

"You don't dream about having a family any longer?"

"I still want that one day, but it's harder to see past everything that has happened."

"What do you mean?"

"It's nothing. Never mind."

He pressed her. "No, tell me."

She'd dated periodically over the years but fear always kept her from allowing a relationship to take a serious turn. Fear that she would mess things up the way she'd let down her friend. But that was something Mike would never understand.

"I've grown confident in my skills as an FBI agent. I know how to deal with things professionally but, personally, I struggle to make the right choice. I still think about that night with Dawn and wish that I had gone with her and how things would be different if I had."

"You should know that second-guessing yourself is a difficult way to live. People make mistakes and you deal with them then move on."

"I know but sometimes consequences are catastrophic. Like what happened to Dawn."

He turned to her and his voice softened. "That wasn't your fault, Christy."

"I was supposed to be with her that night but I chose a boy over my friend. If I'd been there, maybe she would still be alive."

"Or maybe you'd both be missing and there would be no one to look for you."

"People always say that but you don't know it's true. Maybe I could have done something."

"What happened to Dawn wasn't your fault. The blame lies in the person who hurt her. You can't let guilt rule your life. Guilt has no value.

It does nothing to move you forward. It keeps you standing still, stuck where you are. That's no way to live."

A tear streamed down her cheek and she did her best to wipe it away without triggering more. "I know you're right. It's just so hard to get past it."

"Forgiving yourself is the first step, Christy. Letting go of that guilt and moving forward with your life. God isn't the God of guilt. He's the God of redemption and forgiveness. He wants a better life for you and I believe Dawn would have wanted that for you too. She wouldn't have wanted you to live in limbo this way."

His words were soothing to her but why did he have to bring God into this? His mention of God caused her ire to rise. If God didn't want her living this way then why hadn't He acted to save her friend? Bitterness entered her tone as she pushed away from him. "I think what Dawn would have wanted was to live. Why didn't God allow that to happen?"

Disappointment filled his face as he stared at her. Finally, he shook his head. "I don't know the answer to that. But I believe God is good and I trust that He'll reveal the answers to that in His own time."

What had started out as a nice gesture on his

part had turned to heartache because, based on their conversation, she knew the truth. He believed in leaning on God and letting go of guilt, but hers was so permanently embedded inside her that she couldn't see how she would ever overcome it. He wanted a family and kids, but how could she ever find happiness for herself when her friend would never have that opportunity?

His idea of a happy future wasn't possible for Christy.

She took a deep breath and tried to regain her composure. This conversation had gotten way too personal. She wiped the tears from her face and tried to turn the conversation back to the investigation instead. "I think we should focus on finishing these interviews then we can move on."

She could tell he wanted to continue their personal conversation but he finally agreed and took out his list. "We've got two companies left. Weaver's Towing and Langford Towing Company. Weaver's is closer, so we'll go there first."

She nodded. "Do you know either owner?"

"I know them both a little. Weaver's is owned by Rance Weaver. He inherited the business from his brother and sister-in-law, who died in a fire about fifteen years ago. He has one truck and pretty much works on his own. The other is Langford Towing. It's a husband-and-wife team. Chris Langford started the business then brought his wife on board to handle the office and paperwork. They have six drivers. They attend my church and seem like a nice family, but I can't say I really know them all that well."

She made a mental note of his observations. They arrived at Weaver's Towing first and got out. It was a small building with a garage on one side and a large, covered, chain-link fence surrounding the back of the property. The covering blocked her view but, from between the links, she noticed a junkyard full of cars.

A man approached them from the garage, wiping his hands on a rag. "Can I help you?"

Mike showed his badge and Christy offered up her FBI credentials. "We're investigating an old case and wanted to ask you a few questions."

"What's this about?"

"Dawn Cafferty. Did you know her?"

He shook his head. "I don't think so. Why are you questioning me about her?"

"She went missing twelve years ago. We're thinking she was picked up on the side of the road after she had car trouble. Do you have records from then?"

"I don't remember the name but I'll check."

He walked into the small building that held a desk, a file cabinet, a radio, a small sofa against the window and a bathroom off the main room. It was obvious Mr. Weaver only used this building for paperwork and perhaps to stay cool from the afternoon heat. He sat down behind the computer on the desk and tapped in the information for the date Mike had given him.

After a moment, he shook his head. "No, looks like I picked up several calls on the other side of town that night but I wasn't anywhere near Mercy Highway."

Mike glanced out the window at the junkyard. "What about her car? Any chance you found it at a later time and have it back there?"

He typed in the information for the white sedan Dawn had driven. "If I do, it'll be logged in." He shook his head. "No, I don't have any record of the car either." He closed the laptop as he stood. "Sorry I couldn't be more help."

"Thanks for checking." Mike shook his hand then they left and walked back to the SUV. "At least he still had records. Good thing for digital documentation."

"It didn't do us a lot of good," she reminded him.

"I disagree. It helped narrow down where he was and what he was doing. Let's drive over and question the Langfords then we'll head back to the sheriff's office."

They drove for a half hour before Mike pulled into the parking lot of the company. Unlike Weaver, the Langfords had a large building and also rented equipment and moving supplies as well as provided storage units.

Chris Langford greeted them and, after telling him about what they were looking for, he also agreed to check his records. He keyed in the information and pulled up invoices for that time frame when Dawn had gone missing.

"We had three calls that night. Looks like two were picked up and towed to a local garage. The other vehicle was gone before the driver arrived, but the name of the caller was Jenkins, not Cafferty."

"Where was that call supposed to be?"

"South side of the county. Pearson Road."

"That's not far from where Dawn was last seen," Mike told her.

She turned to Langford. "Why wouldn't the car be there when the driver arrived? Does that happen often?"

"It does happen. Sometimes the car starts after they make the call so the driver just heads home and forgets to cancel the truck or someone else stops to help them and gets it moving.

We never really know for sure until we run their credit card and they call back to complain about it. Then we note the reason on the file. Only, I don't see any calls for that date."

Mike glanced at her. "Well, it was worth it to check it out."

She turned to Langford. "Is there ever any tension between you and other towing companies? Do you compete for calls?"

"We have a good working relationship with most of the companies in the area. There's plenty of work for us all. It can happen, though, that a driver comes across a vehicle that's broken down. That's one of the things I was talking about. If someone calls us and a driver from another company arrives on scene before we do, they'll load it up before we arrive."

"Does that happen a lot?"

"Rance Weaver is an independent driver. Sometimes, he'll show up on site before our trucks arrive. I think he drives around looking and waiting for calls."

"We've checked with Weaver. He was on the other side of the county the night in question," Mike explained.

The back door opened and a woman entered. Pretty, with long blond hair, she was wearing sunglasses and carrying a purse and bank bag.

"Sorry," she said. "I just came from the bank. What's going on?"

Her husband answered. "They're looking to see if we picked up that girl who went missing twelve years ago. Remember her?"

"Not really. Did you check the computer?"

"Yeah. We didn't pick her up. I suggested that maybe Rance Weaver came across her."

Christy noticed the woman's polite smile turn guarded. "Yes, that's possible."

"You don't like him, do you?" she asked her. "Why not?"

She did her best to wave away Christy's question. "He's fine. He's just a little brisk and I don't like his tactics. He steals our calls and takes money out of our pockets."

"We don't lose that much money," her husband insisted.

Her nervousness told Christy she couldn't wait to get out of this conversation. She reached into her purse and pulled out her cell phone. "Excuse me. I need to call to check on the kids."

As she stepped away, Langford turned back to them. "My wife isn't as forgiving and forgetting as I am. Sure, Rance has taken a few of our calls before our drivers could get there. That's just business. I don't take it as personally as she does."

Mike thanked him and they each shook his hand before heading out to the SUV.

"Did you notice how Mrs. Langford's demeanor changed when he mentioned Weaver?" Christy asked him as they stepped outside.

Mike either hadn't noticed or didn't seem bothered by it. "I guess she was a little guarded but, like she said, the man undermines her business. I can understand why she wouldn't appreciate that."

"I guess you're right." Although she would have sworn she'd sensed something more by Mrs. Langford's body language. But Mike would know all of them better than she would. Perhaps that behavior was normal for her or she really had been anxious to check on the kids.

"Have we done any criminal background checks on these tow truck drivers? Do any of them have records?"

"Sure, we ran checks on all of them during the original investigation."

"And Rance's came back clean?"

He rubbed the back of his neck as he thought about it. "He didn't have any charges, but a few years later there were some questions emerged about his involvement in his brother's and sister-in-law's deaths."

"Why? Didn't you say they died in a fire?"

"Some people suspected Rance was involved in setting it. It's never been proven, but he did inherit the business and all the land his brother owned."

Another reason for Mrs. Langford not to like him.

"Let's see if he's had any criminal involvement since."

"You think he might have been involved?"

She sighed then rubbed her forehead as a nagging headache reemerged. "I don't know. It's just a feeling. There was something about him that I didn't care for. And being the only employee means he could adjust those logs in any way he wanted to."

Mike agreed to run his background again then they climbed into his SUV.

"Let's head back to the sheriff's office. We'll look at the overall case and see where we're at."

He started the truck then headed toward town.

Car trouble had always been a theory in Dawn's disappearance but, as they'd learned today, there were no records from the towing companies that she'd called for assistance, and Charlie's analysis hadn't found a call for help either.

Someone could have still picked her up off

the side of the road but, with no records and her car still missing, they'd exhausted this lead.

At the sheriff's office, Mike pulled up the criminal record for Rance Weaver. "Looks like he's had a few citations and arrests. Mostly misdemeanor charges for assault and reckless behavior."

"So nothing to indicate he's a predator who abducts and murders young women?" She sighed as he shook his head. That would have been too easy. "Okay then. I think I'll spend the rest of the afternoon looking through these other missing women's files and see if I can find any patterns or connections that might link them to Dawn's case."

He nodded but glanced at his cell phone and his brows narrowed. "Cliff is going before the judge in an hour. I think I'll head over there." He glanced at her. "You okay with that?"

It touched her that he asked. She placed her hand on his. "It's okay, Mike. He's your cousin. I know you care about him."

"It's not just that. I'm sure Rebecca and my aunt will be there as well. They might not want to see me since I'm the one who arrested Cliff, but I should be there for them regardless."

His compassion moved her. He was always thinking of others. "Go. I'll be fine here."

"I won't be long," he assured her before hurrying from the conference room.

She smiled as he left. The man was a bundle of kindness and protective instincts rolled into a very attractive package. She didn't understand how he wasn't married with kids of his own by now, especially since he'd mentioned how much he wanted that.

She wished he was married then that would keep her mind from drifting in his direction.

Christy pulled the case files toward her. She had to stop thinking of Mike that way. Even if she could get past her guilt and fear of messing up and the fact that his cousin probably killed her friend, it still wouldn't work between them. Mike was a small-town guy and she could never live in the town where her friend was murdered. Besides, the last time she'd checked, there were no FBI offices anywhere near Mercy for her to work at.

She turned her attention to the cases of the other three missing women from Mercy County. She tended to immediately discount the Carla Denton case as being connected to Dawn's. Christy's experience told her the deputies were probably right about Carla's son and daughter-in-law having a hand in her disappearance. She'd worked a few cases where family members went missing. Having her only living relatives not report her missing, and then not even bother to call the police for an update on her case, were two red flags that they didn't expect her to return home and weren't interested in trying to find her body. She jotted down a few notes for the investigators to follow up on then put that case aside.

She also agreed with the investigators' initial belief that Shirley Morton's disappearance was likely not a result of foul play. The circumstances of her case were similar to Dawn's but the age difference was troubling. Dawn had been a young, twenty-year-old while Shirley Morton had been a grandmother with health problems. The age of predators, if that was what this was in Dawn's case, might change, but their preference in victims generally didn't. She thought Mrs. Morton might one day be found but doubted her disappearance had any connection to Dawn's.

Christy had a more difficult time dismissing Denise Fields's case however. She'd been a similar age to Dawn and had gone missing only two years prior to Dawn's case. It was Investigation 101 to look at the boyfriend or spouse of women who'd gone missing because, statistically, they presented the biggest threat.

However, by reading through her file, Denise's boyfriend had had no history of violence before or since and his family had always maintained that he was with them. Like Dawn's case, with such little evidence, the police hadn't been able to prove the boyfriend was responsible. Even finding her body hadn't produced the evidence they'd needed to tie him to the murder. Like Cliff, he'd always maintained his innocence but had left town a year after her body was discovered to avoid the speculation and accusations about his involvement.

Was it possible the same killer had been responsible for both women's murders? And she was referring to Dawn's case as a murder despite not having a body. She had no doubt her friend was dead. She couldn't prove it yet but she would.

She sighed and rubbed her head again as the headache grew. She glanced at her watch and decided it was time to call it a day. They'd gotten no further in figuring out this case and her body was already complaining. She had no choice but to take some time to rest.

With Mike in court for his cousin's initial hearing, she asked another deputy to drive her to her hotel, which he did. Steve was working the front desk and saw her struggling with the box of files she'd brought with her. She should have asked the deputy to carry it for her but she hadn't wanted to seem weak in front of him. She still had a reputation she needed to uphold. However, she was tired, bone-tired, and it was taking its toll on her body.

Steve hurried over and took the box. "I'll carry this for you," he told her, easily slipping it under one arm then pressing the elevator button.

"I appreciate that."

"No problem. It's my job to serve the clientele. Have you had any updates on the case?"

"A few," she told him. She didn't normally chat about open cases she was working on yet she didn't want to be rude to someone who'd just come to her rescue either.

"I heard you arrested Cliff Tyner. I always suspected he was involved somehow."

"Why's that?"

"It's always the boyfriend, isn't it? I watch enough true crime TV shows to know that."

She let that slide as the elevator doors slid open. Steve carried the box while she used her keycard to open the door and step inside. "Just place that on the end of the bed," she instructed him.

He set it down then turned to go but stopped and bent to pick up something from the floor.

"What's this? Some kind of note?" He glanced at it then handed it to her. "Someone must have slipped this beneath your door."

Christy took the piece of paper and read it.

I know who killed Dawn. Meet me at Ninth and West Monroe at 9:00 p.m.

She looked up at Steve and felt every muscle in her body tense. This could be the answer she was searching for...or it could be a trap. "I need to see those video feeds. I want to know who slipped this under my door and when."

Mike leaned against the side wall by the door where prisoners were ushered in and out of court. He watched as Cliff took his turn to stand in front of the judge and the charges were read out. Mike cringed at each one. The judge issued a bail amount then called the next case.

His cousin turned and hugged Rebecca, who was sitting in the front row with Aunt Peggy. She whispered something to him then glanced back at Mike, anger flaring in her eyes. As the deputy on duty led Cliff away, Rebecca marched over to Mike and slapped his cheek.

The deputy with Cliff started to react but Mike held up his hand, letting him know it was okay.

"You shouldn't be here, Mike. You should be ashamed of yourself."

Cliff called over to her. "Don't blame him, Rebecca. This isn't his fault." He turned to Mike. "I'm sorry about that. She's just upset."

"It's okay," Mike assured them both. "I understand this isn't easy."

Aunt Peggy linked her arm with Rebecca's and tried to move her on. "Come on, dear. Let's go pay the bail so we can get Cliff home."

Mike rubbed his cheek, which still stung. He hated to think that his aunt was going to pay a hefty sum to get Cliff out of jail and he especially didn't like being on either Rebecca's or his aunt's bad side. They had to know he was there for the family no matter what. He wanted to go to them and offer to take care of the financial aspect but it didn't seem appropriate to do so.

Lord, how did everything get so messed up?

His cell phone buzzed and he glanced at the message from Christy that included a photo of a note.

Received this note under my door. Need to talk ASAP.

He read the words then grimaced. An anonymous note. A meeting in the middle of nowhere at night. It all stank of an ambush.

He texted back that he was on his way then went to find his cousin. This meeting sounded like it was going to get ugly and he wanted to make certain Cliff wasn't pulled into it. Now that he was making bail, he needed to make sure his cousin's movements could be accounted for at all times.

He found him in a waiting cell as Rebecca and Aunt Peggy arranged to pay Cliff's bail.

"What do you want, Mike?" Cliff asked him, not even bothering to stand to greet him.

"I need you to do something for me, Cliff," he said. "Once you're released, I need you to stay at the house with Rebecca and the girls. Don't leave. Don't go anywhere."

"You want me to be a prisoner in my own home now? You can't make me do that."

"I know I can't, that's why I'm asking you to do it. Look, I have to take care of something and, if I'm right, it might turn ugly, but it also might be something that helps clear your name. But only if you do as I ask and stay at the house until you hear from me again."

His curiosity piqued, Cliff stood and walked to the cell door. "What's happening?"

"I can't tell you that. Just stay at the house until I call you back. Will you do that?"

Cliff agreed. "Yeah. I had no plans of going out tonight anyway. I doubt Rebecca will let me out of her sight."

Mike felt better knowing that Cliff would be out of the line of fire. He hoped to talk Christy out of going to this meeting but he knew her well enough now to know that she would want to go and see for herself whether or not whoever had written the note had any information to give them.

Of course, he was right.

He arrived at her hotel and she opened the door, already pumped and ready to go. "Oh, good. It was getting late. I didn't think you were going to make it."

He walked in and closed the door behind him, hoping to appeal to her sense of reason. It didn't help that she was checking her gun while he was talking.

"You can't go," he said. "This note is suspicious. You do realize that, right?"

"I know it's a risk but I can't not go, either, can I?"

"A random person slips a note under your door, claiming to have all the answers you've been looking for, but instead of coming to the sheriff's office or calling you, they want a face-to-face meeting at night in the middle of no-where? Christy, this can't be legit. How did they even know what room you were in?"

She hesitated only for a moment but at least that was something. Then she shook away her doubts. "I don't know, Mike. I just know I'm going and I don't want to go alone."

He sighed. "There's not enough time to get a team together."

"I don't need a team of sheriff's office deputies. That might frighten this person off. I need you for backup, Mike, just in case. If there's a chance that this person, whoever it is, actually knows what happened to Dawn, then I have to take the risk."

She closed the distance between them and touched his arm, her eyes pleading with him. "Please, Mike. Please come with me."

He'd known coming in that he wasn't going to talk her out of this, yet he'd had to try. And he certainly wasn't going to allow her to go alone. As she stared up at him with pleading eyes, he wondered if there was anything he would deny her. He reached and moved a strand of hair from her face, his hand gently brushing her cheek. He shuddered at the softness of her skin. How had this woman become so important to him so fast? He didn't know but he wasn't going to let anything happen to her until he could figure it out.

"Okay," he finally agreed. "But at the first sign of trouble, I'm calling in backup." He would have his team gathering on alert and ready to act, certain they would need them if the person who had sent that note actually showed up.

A smile broke through the gloom on her face. "Thank you." She kissed his cheek, causing his face to warm at the feeling, then went back to checking her weapon. "Are you armed?" she asked, obviously referring to something other than the Glock visible on his hip.

He nodded. "I've got tactical gear in the SUV." It should be more than adequate to keep her safe during her meetup and his rifle meant he could watch the scene and provide cover from a distance.

Still, he pulled out his cell phone and dialed the sheriff's office, speaking with Deputy Josh Knight who oversaw and planned most of the office's tactical missions. He agreed to do his best to pull a small team together to have at the ready in case there was trouble.

Mike thanked him then ended the call and turned to Christy, who returned her now-cleaned weapon to its holster then zipped her jacket to conceal it.

He sent up a silent prayer for God's guidance and protection then led her down to the SUV and braced himself for what was to come.

Even if this was an ambush, and it surely was, if they could turn the tables and capture the assailant, they could end this once and for all.

Ninth and West Monroe was nothing but a barren street corner with a stop sign and an abandoned gas station. No houses were visible but Christy could hear the roar of a train in the near distance.

She tapped the earbud that was connected to her open cell phone line. She felt better knowing that Mike was close, watching her and waiting to act, and this time she was prepared for the worst with her gun at the ready. "How close is that train?" she asked Mike, who was nearby observing and covering her.

"Pretty close," he responded. "Just down the road. I don't see anyone approaching yet."

She checked her watch. It was already twenty past nine. The anonymous letter writer was late. Had he seen Mike's presence and changed his mind about coming? Or had this been only one big distraction?

"Wait, I've got someone approaching from the east on foot."

She tensed and longed to reach for her weapon but she didn't want to scare the person off. She turned in the direction he'd stated and spotted a teenager carrying a backpack heading her way. He shot her a curious glance as he turned before he reached her then darted down the street.

She relaxed a bit. "That wasn't him," she told Mike. "Just a kid probably on his way home." She checked the time again and sighed. "I'm not sure anyone is coming." She'd expected this to be a trap of some sort at the very least, but it appeared to be nothing more than a prank. No one was coming to meet her.

"Hold on," Mike said through the earbud, his voice terse. "Get down," he shouted moments before she heard the tat-tat-tat of gunfire.

She dropped to the ground just as something whizzed past her head and she realized the gunfire wasn't coming only from Mike's rifle. Someone was shooting at her.

EIGHT

She pulled her gun then spun around, trying to find the shooter as she hurried to take cover against the wall of the abandoned building. She scanned the area but she saw nothing.

"Where is he?" she cried.

Suddenly, movement from the bushes across the street grabbed her attention as a figure darted out and took off running.

"I've got him," she cried into the phone as she ran after the assailant.

He was fast, sprinting between trees and over fences and cutting through yards. Christy kept him in sight then realized Mike was coming up behind her, running much faster than she could.

"Where is he?" he asked her.

"There!" She pointed to the fleeing figure and Mike took off.

She kept up with him, making sure to keep

them both in her line of sight. Mike was the quicker runner. If either of them was going to catch up to the shooter, it would be him.

The clang of the train grew louder the farther they ran and she realized the shooter was heading for the tracks. The train was already rolling through and she could see the guy was making a run for an open railway car.

"Stop," Mike shouted after him.

Instead, the guy turned around, raised his gun and fired.

Christy returned fire and so did Mike. The guy stumbled then recovered but she still wasn't close enough with the pall of darkness to see his face.

He reached the boxcar and hopped onto the train and Mike ran after him. Christy did her best to keep up but the train pulled farther and farther away. Finally, Mike stopped chasing, too, and leaned over to catch his breath as Christy caught up to him.

He pulled out his cell phone and dialed the sheriff's office. "We have a suspect that just hopped into a boxcar on the outbound train. We need to stop it as soon as possible." He ended the call then turned to her. "Let's head back to the SUV. Maybe we can catch up with it."

She agreed and they ran back to where he'd

parked his vehicle. "I think I hit him," Christy said as they climbed inside.

At least, she hoped so. She'd hit the man who'd run her off the road, too, and they hadn't been able to find him yet. Plus, she'd had a better shot for that incident.

Mike's radio was lighting up with activity as they got into his SUV and followed the path of the tracks until they saw the train stopped several miles down the line. Multiple sheriff's office vehicles were parked nearby and they were already searching each car for the suspect. Mike hopped out and Christy followed him. The deputy in charge approached him. "Looks like the suspect jumped out somewhere between where you encountered him and here. We're still searching, but we did find some blood in one of the boxcars."

Mike headed over to where he'd motioned and Christy hurried behind him. He climbed into the boxcar before turning to help Christy hop into the train car. His team had already marked the spot where they'd found blood. He bent down to look at it then up at her. "Guess you were right. You did hit him."

She nodded then turned to the other deputy in the car. "Put out an alert at the local hospital and medical centers. I want to be notified if anyone comes in with a gunshot wound."

The deputy pulled out his phone to make the call.

Mike stood and turned to her. "At least we know there's someone else targeting you. I made sure my cousin had an alibi. I don't want him mixed up in this."

She knew Cliff had made bail earlier and could see Mike was itching to phone him. "For what it's worth, I don't think it was Cliff we were chasing, but go ahead and call him to make sure."

He walked away from the scene and took out his cell phone as Christy surveyed the area. Mike had been right about this being an ambush, but she hadn't wanted to listen to him. She'd been so determined to do whatever it took to find answers that she hadn't used her better judgment. She thought about how close that bullet had come to her head and shuddered. She'd very nearly paid the price for her headstrongness.

She glanced over at Mike as he groaned in frustration. "Everything okay?"

He shook his head. "He's not answering his cell. I'm calling Rebecca."

He made the call and she obviously picked up. "Rebecca. Where's Cliff? I can't reach him."

Christy watched his face fall with disappointment and felt it herself. With his cousin out on the streets, they had to consider him a suspect. Why hadn't he stayed put like Mike had asked him to?

"How long has he been gone?" He closed his eyes then he sighed at her answer. "A few hours? Call me the minute he shows back up."

"He's not there?" she asked when he ended the call.

He shook his head. "He left not long after he got home." He gripped the phone tighter, glanced around at the crime scene and shook his head.

Christy touched his arm then couldn't resist pulling him into a hug.

He wrapped his arms around her and held on tightly before releasing her. He gave her a nod of thanks. "I just hope when he shows back up that he isn't sporting a gunshot wound."

For Mike's sake, she hoped the same.

Mike finished clearing the scene, overseeing the collection of the blood and any cameras in the area. He was doubtful of finding any. Like Christy, he hadn't gotten a good look at the shooter but his fear had been realized. Whoever had sent that note had meant to kill her.

His heart had been racing ninety to nothing nonstop since the shooting. Everything had gone wrong tonight. They should have captured this guy and then everything would have been over. Only, he'd gotten away from them again.

He tried his cousin's phone again, growing angrier with each unanswered call. He couldn't wait to drop Christy off so he could hunt down Cliff and demand answers.

He drove Christy to her hotel and walked her upstairs to her room.

She turned to him before he left. "I'm sorry about your cousin, Mike. I hope you find him and that he's okay."

He appreciated that she cared. He reached out and touched her cheek and she leaned into his hand. He couldn't remember when she'd become important to him but she had. He couldn't see any way that it could work between them unless they could find the real perpetrator.

"Be careful," she told him. "And let me know what happens."

"I will."

He pulled himself away from her and left, driving to his cousin's house. His truck was gone but that didn't stop Mike from knocking on the door and pushing his way inside when Rebecca opened it.

"Where is he?"

"He's not here," Rebecca stated. "I told you that on the phone."

"Have you heard from him since we spoke? Where is he?"

"I don't know," she insisted. "I haven't seen or heard from him for hours. What's the matter, Mike? Is he in trouble again?"

"I don't know. Maybe. He was supposed to remain here so he wouldn't be." Frustration railed through him. Why couldn't Cliff just do the right thing for once?

Tears streamed down Rebecca's face. "He was so upset when he left. He told me he wouldn't be home for a long time. He thinks he's going to jail, Mike. He believes you're going to send him away for hurting Dawn. Please, Mike, you have to help him."

Mike stared at her. Cliff was scared but was that because he knew he'd been caught or just worry that the evidence appeared to point to him? "If he did this, Rebecca, then he will go to jail. There's nothing I can do to stop that."

But first, he had to find him.

By the next morning, there was still no sign of Cliff Tyner. Mike was scouring the town looking for him and Christy didn't begrudge him that task. She, too, wished that Cliff had remained at home like Mike had asked him to. If it turned out his cousin was the one who'd tried to ambush them, then that would turn their situation on its head.

Christy decided to spend the day at the hotel rereading through the notes of the case. She needed to make some headway but she also needed rest. Her body was crying out for time to heal and relax after the multiple attacks against her. Only, relaxing wasn't a word in her vocabulary. She compromised with a swim in the hotel pool followed by a long hot shower and room service before she turned her attention back to the case.

She read through the notes from the tow truck drivers but her initial response at reading them was the same as when they'd conducted the interviews. Nothing had stood out.

Then she skimmed through the notes from Langford Towing. The interview hadn't really given them anything yet she recalled how Mrs. Langford's demeanor had changed when they'd started talking about Rance Weaver.

Her reaction still bothered Christy.

She pulled up Weaver's record again but Mike had been correct about his past. Nothing stood out. He had some misdemeanor charges but nothing to make law enforcement believe he was a predator.

Still, it wouldn't hurt to question Mrs. Langford again and discover what had been behind her odd reaction.

She glanced at the time. It was nearing the end of the business day but if she hurried, maybe she could catch the couple heading home after work.

She gathered up her papers then dashed downstairs. She'd called for a cab to drive her to the car rental place and had arranged to have a new rental waiting for her. Once she'd completed the paperwork and had the vehicle, she drove to the address she had on file for the Langford family.

She pulled up just as they were exiting the house. Mr. and Mrs. Langford were hurrying the kids along to the SUV in the driveway.

Mr. Langford greeted her. "Agent Williams, we were just on our way out to grab some take-out. What can we do for you?"

His wife put the kids into the back seat, closed the door then walked over to join the conversation.

"I was actually hoping to speak with you again, Mrs. Langford, about Rance Weaver."

She saw the change in the woman again. She

stiffened and folded her arms in a guarded way. Christy hadn't been wrong about her knowing something. "My husband told you everything. None of our trucks picked up that woman twelve years ago."

"I know that but I can also see there's something else that troubles you about Rance Weaver. Please. A woman is missing. She was my friend. I can tell you know something."

Her husband looked at her then took the keys from her hand. "Why don't me and the kids run through the drive-thru and give you two time to talk?"

She reluctantly nodded then headed back to the porch as her husband and kids drove away. She sat down in a rocker but pulled her sweater tight against her. "Chris told you about Rance Weaver sometimes showing up before our drivers can arrive. Well, I know for a fact he drives around looking for business."

"There's nothing illegal about that."

"No, but even as a teenager, I'd heard stories about him. Picking up girls stranded on the road and forcing them to…" She gulped hard. "Do things to repay him."

Christy tensed. "What kinds of things?"

"He cornered me one night. My car had broken down. I had the baby in the car with me and I was waiting on Chris to come get me. Rance Weaver pulled up first. He tried to get me to call Chris and tell him not to come. He was very insistent and made me extremely uncomfortable. He pressed me against the car." Tears formed in her eyes. "I was terrified of him. I thought he was going to force himself on me. I still remember the weight of him pressing me against that car."

"But he didn't force you?"

"My husband arrived before he could really do anything. Rance saw the headlights coming and moved away from me. He acted like nothing had happened when Chris arrived. I never told my husband. I was afraid of what he might do to Rance, but I made sure I was never alone with that man again."

Christy zeroed in on something else. "You said you'd heard stories about him. Do you remember any names or places?"

"A few years ago, probably four or five, after this happened, we received a call about a broken-down vehicle. We only had two drivers at the time, my husband being one of them. He took the call but when he arrived, the car was already gone."

Christy nodded. "Yes, your husband said that happens sometimes."

"Right, so neither of us thought anything about it. Only, the next morning, the car was sitting in our lot. Also, that morning, I received a call from a woman who was beside herself with anger. She said the driver who towed her car tried to attack her daughter. After he'd already loaded the car and she was in the cab of his truck, he told her that she had to pay him and when she insisted her parents had already paid with a credit card, he insisted that he wanted a different form of payment. She tried to accuse my husband. I knew it had to have been Rance but I couldn't prove it. I assured her it wasn't our driver and told her she needed to call the police, but she didn't want to make a police report. She didn't want her daughter to have to testify against this man. I couldn't blame her. He's crazy. He burned down that house with his brother and sister-in-law inside it. There's no telling what he'll do."

Her story sounded like something that might have happened to Dawn. Only, she hadn't made it out alive. Had Rance Weaver killed her to keep her quiet about his actions? And how many others had he done the same thing to but they were also too scared to come forward?

Christy took down Mrs. Langford's statement then asked her for the name of the family.

She didn't even have to look it up. She knew it from memory. "I see them sometimes around town and I've seen write-ups about their daughter. I believe she's in college now and doing well."

"I'll call them and see if they corroborate your story."

"If they didn't want to file a police report then what makes you think they'll want to talk to you now?" Mrs. Langford asked.

"The daughter would have been a teenager then. She'll be grown now. Maybe she wants to tell her story finally." She seemed to have her doubts, but Christy had to try. "Thank you for telling me this."

"Of course, I can't prove anything I've just told you."

Christy shook her head then leaned over and touched Mrs. Langford's hand. "You don't have to prove it. That's my job."

She waited until Mr. Langford and the kids returned then watched as Mrs. Langford joined her family in heading inside. She overheard her husband ask what Christy had wanted and Mrs. Langford waved off his question. She'd obviously done a good job of keeping her husband in the dark about what had happened with Rance Weaver. He suspected nothing.

She pulled out her cell phone and looked up the name Mrs. Langford had given her. Joanna Middleton. A quick call to the sheriff's office and she had an address that wasn't too far away. She decided showing up in person would be her best option. This family had held back this story for years. They certainly weren't going to confess their darkest secrets to her over the telephone.

She pulled up to the address located in a nicer area of town. A far cry nicer than the area where Tony Freely's house was and where she'd nearly been shot on Ninth. She got out, walked to the front door and knocked.

A middle-aged woman with a big smile answered. "Yes, can I help you?"

Christy showed the woman her FBI credentials. "My name is special agent Christy Williams of the FBI. I'm in town working a missing persons case. Maybe you've heard of it? Dawn Cafferty? She disappeared twelve years ago."

She bobbed her head. "Yes, of course I've heard of her."

"I understand you have some information about an incident with your daughter involving a man named Rance Weaver. I was hoping I could talk with you about it."

Her brow creased into a frown. "I don't know

what I can tell you. The man is a predator. He tried to attack my daughter and all he got was a slap on the wrist."

Her words didn't make any sense to Christy. "What do you mean he got a slap on the wrist?"

"The prosecutor pled his case down to a misdemeanor assault and all he got was community service. That man attacked my daughter but he was treated as if he'd gotten into a bar fight. It was humiliating."

Christy recalled seeing the misdemeanor assault charge on his criminal history but she hadn't connected it to a sexual assault. "I was under the impression that you didn't press charges against him."

"Well, I didn't want to, but my daughter insisted. She wanted to get that man off the streets. A lot of good it did us. My daughter was retraumatized by the system."

Christy jotted down the information. She was going to have to go back and look further into the case to find out more documented details. It was possible Mercy had a serial predator who had gotten away with his trade for far too long.

Unlike Mrs. Langford had insisted, Joanna Middleton was happy to give her details of what had happened to her daughter and they

matched up to what the other woman had told
her. Weaver had come across the broken-down
vehicle at night with a woman alone and tried
to assault her once he had her vulnerable and
alone in his cab. Mrs. Middleton's daughter had
been fortunate to escape, yet Christy couldn't
help but wonder if the same thing had happened to Dawn. She hadn't been so fortunate.

It would certainly explain why there was no
cell phone call for a tow truck and why the vehicle was missing. As Mike had said, hiding
a car in a tow yard would be an easy way to
make it disappear for good.

She thanked Mrs. Middleton then left.

"I hope you get him off the street," the lady
said before Christy left.

Christy turned and glanced at her. She looked
like a woman who had been put through the
ringer. Her daughter had been through a terrible tragedy and she hadn't been able to protect
her. Only a glimmer of hope was left behind
her cynical expression.

"I will," she promised. She was not only
doing this for Dawn now. She was doing this
for all the women who hadn't found justice for
Rance Weaver's actions.

She headed back to the sheriff's office and
requested the full file on the assault case in-

volving Rance Weaver. She also wanted to know how many other complaints there had been against him.

While she waited for the file, she printed off photos of Cliff, Rance Weaver and some other men with physical similarities. Tony Freely's testimony that he'd seen Cliff pushing Dawn into his pickup the night she'd vanished was a hurdle she needed to overcome before turning her sights on Rance Weaver. She hadn't realized it before, but Cliff and Weaver had similar body types. She wondered if Freely could have been mistaken in his identification. He'd seemed sincere but it wouldn't be the first time eyewitness testimony had been mistaken. Also, it was possible Freely had told her what she'd wanted to hear just to get a plea deal. His word was unreliable, so she needed to test that identification with a lineup. They'd gotten caught up in other things and hadn't done one yet.

She phoned and asked that Freely be brought to an interview room and she presented him with the photo lineup. "Can you identify the man you saw pushing Dawn Cafferty into his truck the night she disappeared?"

Freely picked up the array and scanned through the photos. After a moment, confusion clouded his expression. "I thought it was this guy," he said, pointing to Cliff. "Now I'm wondering if it wasn't this guy." He pointed to Rance Weaver.

"Take another look," Christy told him. "Do your best to remember."

He rubbed a hand over his hair as he stared at the photos then shook his head. "I'm not sure anymore."

It had been a risk presenting him with this photo lineup since she had just undermined the case against Cliff while not even securing a solid identification on Weaver. She thanked Freely for trying then sent him back to his cell.

A deputy stopped her and handed her a file. "I was just bringing this to the conference room. It's the file you requested."

"Thanks. I'll take it. I'm heading back to my hotel, if Mike or anyone needs me."

She took the file with her to her hotel and poured through it, shocked to find how detailed the case seemed. The victim's statement was concise and thorough; there were even photos of Amber Middleton's injuries as she'd attempted to flee the cab of Rance Weaver's tow truck. The sheriff's office had even managed to obtain GPS information to prove that his truck had been in the same vicinity where the attack had taken place. It looked like the sheriff's office had done its job. Yet somehow the case had fallen apart sometime before it reached trial.

Someone had dropped the ball and allowed a predator back on the streets of Mercy.

NINE

Relief flooded Mike when he received the call from the bartender at McClain's to let him know his cousin had showed up there earlier. It was the first sign of Cliff since he'd gone dark the night before.

He hadn't technically done anything to break his bail but he'd promised Mike he would remain at home and he'd broken that promise. It wasn't the first time he'd been his own worst enemy but, this time, it was messing with Mike's investigation too.

He drove by McClain's and spotted Cliff's truck parked in the lot. Hopefully, he'd been there since he'd left home and had a bar full of witnesses who could corroborate that. He walked inside and scanned the room but saw no sign of his cousin.

Jerry sat at the bar and turned to him when Mike approached. "He was here earlier," he told him. "But he left about a half hour ago."

"How long was he here? When did he arrive?"

"I don't know. He called me and I agreed to meet him here but then he stormed out. He was real upset. He's afraid of going to prison for something he didn't do."

If he was so worried, then he should have stayed at home the way Mike had asked him to do. "His truck is still parked in the lot."

Jerry shrugged. "I'm telling you he left a while ago."

"When did he call you? What time did you arrive here?"

"It hasn't been long. An hour or so ago."

Mike rubbed his face. So, once again, his cousin didn't have an alibi at the time of the ambush. "Did he look like he had any injuries?"

Jerry turned and took a sip of his drink, hesitating, and Mike got a bad feeling.

"Jerry, was he hurt?"

He nodded. "He had blood on his pants and he was walking with a limp. He said he'd done something he wished he hadn't done."

That sounded an awful lot like a confession. "Did he say what?"

"No. He just got up and left. Said he had to make things right."

Yet his truck was still in the parking lot.

Mike walked outside to the truck. He shined

a flashlight in the truck and spotted blood on the seat, but Cliff wasn't in it. He realized Jerry had followed him out of the bar.

"He must be around here somewhere," Jerry stated, a troubling look of concern on his face.

They both scanned the area. Mike walked to the rear of the building. It backed up to a wooded lot once the blacktop ended. He strained his ears and swore he heard something. It sounded like crying and it was coming from the woods.

Mike followed the sound. "Cliff, Cliff, is that you?"

He heard noises and walked closer until he detected the click of a gun. That stopped him in his tracks and his hand immediately went to his own weapon.

"Don't come any closer."

He recognized Cliff's voice and spotted him a moment later. He was holding a gun, but he wasn't pointing it toward Mike. Crouched against a tree, he was holding the gun to his head.

Mike's immediate concerns changed from worry about a threat to his life to the threat to his cousin's. "Cliff, what are you doing?"

"I don't have anything left to live for, Mike. I'm know I'm going to prison. I'm going to prison for something I didn't even do. I'm going to be labeled a murderer and my family is going to be ruined. I can't go through that, Mike."

Mike gritted his teeth as he gave Cliff a quick once-over. He saw blood on his pant leg, just as Jerry had said; probably blood from the same wound that had seeped onto the seat of his truck. He spotted Jerry coming toward them and stopped him, motioning him to call for help. Jerry nodded then hurried off. His cousin was in crisis and Mike needed to talk him down before he did something he couldn't come back from.

Mike crouched down so his cousin would see him as less threatening. "Cliff, is that blood on your pants? Are you hurt?"

"Yeah."

"How'd that happen, Cliff?" His mind was racing back to the train and the blood they'd found there. Was it going to match his cousin's?

Cliff didn't answer his question. Instead, he started crying. "I don't know what to do, Mike. Everything is out of control. I don't want to go to jail."

"You don't have to do this, Cliff. We'll figure this out. If you didn't hurt Dawn, then give me more time to prove it."

"You can't prove it. It's been twelve years and you still can't prove it. And that FBI agent wants me in jail."

"She's only following the evidence, Cliff, but, trust me, she wants to know the truth about what happened to Dawn. She's not looking to put away someone innocent just to close the case. She wants to know the truth."

He shook his head. "No, she blames me. Everyone blames me." He raised the gun and looked intent on using it on himself.

Mike had no choice but to intervene. He closed the distance between them before Cliff could pull the trigger. Mike tackled him, knocking the gun from his grip just as it went off.

Cliff cried out in frustration but didn't try to retrieve it.

Jerry came running back into the clearing. "The ambulance is on the way," he told them. Jerry sat beside his friend and put his arm around him, reassuring him. "It's going to be okay," he told Cliff. "We're going to get you the help you need."

Mike waited until the ambulance arrived and they'd loaded Cliff into it before he headed to his SUV to retrieve an evidence bag. He bagged the gun for processing. They'd located rounds the fleeing figure had fired at him and Christy as they'd chased him and they would need to try to pair them to this gun. He prayed it didn't come back as a match.

Only, despite Cliff's insistence, everything was pointing to him as the culprit and Mike couldn't help but wonder how he could have been so wrong about his cousin all these years.

It was late when Christy received the phone call from Mike about his cousin.

"He wanted to end his life," he told her, his voice full of pain and anguish. "He was so desperate and worried about going to jail that he was ready to end his life."

Her heart broke for him but they'd both known it wouldn't be easy when and if Cliff finally confessed.

She assured him she was on her way and ran downstairs to her new rental car, climbed inside and headed for the hospital. When she arrived, Mike was sitting with Rebecca and his aunt. He stood and she hurried toward him and pulled him into a hug. His arms encircled her and he clung to her in desperation.

"How is he?" she asked.

"We're still waiting to hear," he said before adding, "They're treating him for a gunshot wound to his leg."

She sighed, understanding his meaning. They'd shot at the man who'd ambushed them at the train tracks and now Cliff had reappeared with a gun wound. It had to have been his cousin who had ambushed her last night and been shot in the process. Despite what she'd learned today about Rance Weaver, it seemed obvious that Cliff had been the one trying to stop her investigation and, when it hadn't worked, he'd tried to end his life instead of going to prison for Dawn's murder. Only, there were still questions that needed to be answered. Who, for instance, had run her off the road while Cliff was sitting in jail?

"Have you spoken to him?" she asked. She hadn't wanted to press him over the phone for what Cliff had said to him during their standoff in the woods, but it sounded like he might have been close to confessing what he'd done.

Mike shook his head. "No, they're not allowing anyone in to see him at the moment." He glanced over her head. "There's the doctor."

He motioned for Rebecca and his aunt to join him as the doctor approached with an update. "Are you the Tyner family?"

"We are," Rebecca insisted. "I'm his wife. How is he?"

"We've sedated him for the moment. We had to treat a gunshot wound to his leg and he was extremely agitated. He'll be fine, but we'll see how he's doing when he wakes up."

"Can I stay with him?" she asked.

The doctor gave a slight shrug. "I'm fine with it, but we'll have to get the okay from the sheriff's office since they brought him in."

"I'll get it approved," Mike assured him. "He's technically out on bail, so he's not under arrest, but I want to leave a deputy on his door."

Christy could have argued that his bail could be revoked for having a weapon, but she wasn't going to press that issue since Mike was requesting a deputy to watch him. He wasn't going anywhere without them being alerted first.

"We need to speak with him," she told the doctor, pulling out her FBI credentials and showing them to him. "It's part of a missing persons investigation."

"He'll be out for a while and I'm not sure a police interrogation is what he needs at the moment."

She didn't miss the glare Rebecca sent her way, yet she pressed on. "It's very important," she insisted, but the doctor was firm.

"He's resting. Maybe you can interview him in the morning."

He was adamant in his refusal and Christy could tell no amount of insisting was going to change his mind. She was disappointed.

"We'll talk to him tomorrow," Mike stated. They watched as Rebecca followed the doctor down to the last room on the hallway.

Mike pulled on her arm and led her away from his aunt. "What are you doing? What was that?"

"I just thought he sounded like he was ready to confess back there in the woods. I believe he's ready to tell the truth about what happened the night Dawn vanished. We need to press him for a confession and answers."

He stared at her for a moment then pulled a hand through his hair and shot her a frustrated look. "This is my town, Christy. These are my people. I care about them, even my cousin. Murderer or not, he's still family."

"Family who shot at us, or have you forgotten?"

"You don't know it was him."

She was stunned by his response. "Your cousin wasn't where he was supposed to be, plus he's spotting a gunshot wound just like the man we chased. I understand you want to believe in your cousin, Mike, but you can't really believe it wasn't him, can you?"

She could see the doubt still in his face. "I don't know what I believe yet."

She shook her head in disbelief. His devotion

to his family had been admirable once upon a time, but how long could someone really ignore what was right in front of their eyes?

"You're letting your personal feelings cloud your judgment."

"And you're determined to convict Cliff no matter what. When you arrived, you made me promise that I wouldn't allow you to have tunnel vision. Well, guess what, you have it. It's not so cut and dried, Christy. Cliff was sitting in jail when you were run off the road. How do you account for that?"

"I can't, but I don't have to. I have his lies, his messages to arrange a meeting with Dawn, and an eyewitness who saw him pushing her into his pickup, and now this. I might not be able to prove that he was the one who conducted these attacks against me, but I do have enough to put him away for murder."

She didn't tell him what she'd uncovered about Rance Weaver or how she'd tainted Freely's identification of Cliff because the gunshot wound seemed to prove Cliff's involvement. And, tomorrow, once he was awake, she would make him admit it.

"Maybe once you hear the truth from his own mouth, you'll be able to accept it."

"I guess we'll know tomorrow then, won't

we?" He'd clung to her only minutes ago but now his tone had turned cold. He turned and walked away from her, rejoining his aunt in the waiting room. It was obvious from his body language that he wasn't going to invite her to stay.

Tomorrow they would have answers.

She stopped by the nurses' station and left her name and number, asking to be alerted if there was a change in Cliff's status. The nurse agreed but only because she flashed her FBI credentials. She didn't know if she would be given a call but she'd done what she could.

She left the hospital, glad she'd driven her new rental car and wasn't dependent upon Mike to drive her to the hotel. But she couldn't stop the tears that pressed against her eyes as she slid behind the wheel. She'd allowed herself to fall for Mike and that had been a mistake.

Small towns were notorious for closing in on outsiders and she suspected that was what was happening here. She didn't believe Mike was intentionally covering for his cousin, but his inactions were giving him an out. Hopefully, tomorrow, Cliff would finally confess what he'd done and Christy could leave this town, and Mike, behind once and for all.

She pulled into the parking lot at the hotel

then parked. She couldn't wait to get a hot shower and try to sleep and wipe away the ickiness of this day. She was already tired and morning was only a few hours away. She planned to be at the hospital bright and early so she didn't miss her opportunity to question Cliff.

She slid out of the car and closed the door but the key fob slipped from her hand and onto the pavement. She knelt to get them then stood and saw a figure in the reflection from the window standing behind her.

The man clamped something over her mouth before she could even react or scream for help. He pinned her arms and held her, forcing her to breathe in something that was on the rag. She held her breath for as long as she could but finally succumbed to it. The ground seemed to move beneath her and darkness threatened the edges of her vision. The man opened the car door and pushed her inside, over the console and into the passenger's seat. She slammed into the glass but hardly felt it as her stomach rolled and darkness threatened to pull her under from whatever agent he'd dosed her with.

He pulled away from the hotel and, without the ability to fight, she closed her eyes and surrendered to the darkness.

TEN

Mike couldn't bring himself to leave the hospital and go home, but he did convince his aunt to go by promising to phone her if something changed. He'd only convinced her to leave by reminding her that with Rebecca remaining overnight, his nieces were being watched by a neighbor.

He drove her to Cliff and Rebecca's house but it didn't feel right staying there after what he'd done by arresting Cliff. The family couldn't really blame him for Cliff's breakdown but he wasn't anybody's favorite person at the moment.

Especially not Christy's.

He hated the way they'd argued, but she had her mind set that Cliff was guilty. He knew it didn't look good for his cousin yet he wasn't ready to say for sure without further evidence. He was sure tomorrow she wasn't going to hold herself back from demanding answers.

Still, he couldn't get out of his head how Cliff had insisted he was going to prison for something he *hadn't* done. That hadn't sounded like a confession to him but an insistence that he was innocent.

He returned to the hospital, grabbed some coffee from the vending machine then propped up his legs on a chair and did his best to sleep.

Around 6:00 a.m., someone tapped on his shoulder. He opened his eyes to see Jerry and Devon standing there.

"We wanted to drop by before work to see how Cliff is doing," Jerry told him.

Mike stood up to greet them then filled them in on what he knew, which wasn't much.

Devon shook his head. "I wish I'd been there for him. I had a missed call from him but I was already asleep when he phoned."

"I'm not sure there was much you could have done," Jerry told him and Mike agreed.

"Cliff was out of his head with grief. He wasn't thinking clearly."

"What'll happen to him now?" Devon asked Mike.

He shrugged, uncertain. "He'll need to answer some questions. Christy and I were lured to a meeting last night and someone shot at her. We fired back and hit the assailant. The fact that Cliff has no alibi and a gunshot wound means he's got a lot of explaining to do about that." He glanced at his watch. "In fact, Christy will probably be by in an hour or so to start demanding answers."

"You're in a tough spot, aren't you?" Devon asked him.

His question caught Mike off guard for a moment but it felt good to have someone else acknowledge that. "Yeah. The family is pretty upset with me. They blame me for arresting him."

Both men shook their heads. "You had a job to do," Devon insisted. "Even Cliff knew that. They'll come around to realizing that too."

Jerry patted his arm. "I know Cliff pretty well and I don't believe he's been doing these attacks against you and Agent Williams, but it's not my job to figure this out. It's yours. He's definitely had something bugging him for years. His drinking has gotten worse since I've known him. He's been struggling with something."

Mike knew that was true but he'd always assumed it was the cloud of suspicion that had hovered over him all these years.

Movement down the hallway grabbed Mike's

attention. He looked up to see Rebecca walking toward them. He stood. "How is he?"

"He's awake and feeling better," she said.

"Can we see him?" Jerry asked. "We won't stay long."

She smiled at the other two men then glared at Mike. "He'll be happy to see you both." She turned and led Jerry and Devon down the hallway, leaving Mike standing there alone.

He didn't object. He would have his chance to speak with Cliff. It wouldn't hurt to give him a few good moments before the conversation turned to not-so-pleasant things.

He glanced at his watch, surprised Christy hadn't arrived yet. He decided to call her to let her know Cliff was awake and able to see them. Her cell phone rang continuously but she didn't pick up. He didn't bother leaving a voicemail. She would know why he was calling and would either return the call or show up at the hospital.

Devon and Jerry stayed for only a few minutes then left to go to work, stopping by to let Mike know that Cliff looked to be in good spirits. He thanked them then sat and waited. He wouldn't press to see Cliff until Christy arrived.

Only, when she hadn't showed up or returned

his call after an hour, he tried her number again. Again, there was no answer.

After another hour of no contact, he grew worried. At first, he'd assumed she was not responding because she was still fuming at him after their dust-up the previous evening.

Only now it was after nine and she hadn't arrived or called to say she was on her way.

No way she would miss the opportunity to question Cliff about his involvement. She'd been so certain his cousin was ready to spill his guts about his involvement in Dawn's disappearance, she wouldn't just not show now. His gut was telling him that something was wrong.

He looked up the number for the hotel and called the front desk. Steve answered, surprising him. "I thought you worked nights."

"Yes, I'm filling in for the daytime clerk who called in sick. What can I do for you, Deputy?"

"Can you connect me to Agent Williams's room? She's not answering her cell phone."

"No problem." He transferred the call but, after multiple rings, the call reverted back to the front desk. "It doesn't look like she's answering. Do you want to leave a message for her?"

"No. Something is wrong. Send someone up

to her room to make certain she's okay. I'm on my way to you now."

"I'll go myself," Steve told him then ended the call.

Mike put on his sirens and drove as fast as possible, making it to the hotel in record time.

He hurried up the stairs, ignoring the elevator that would take too much time to use. He pushed open the hallway door and found Steve waiting by the door to her room. He looked confused.

"What is it?" he asked Steve. Terrible images of what he might have found flickered through his mind but Steve didn't look to be distressed.

"It's nothing. She's not in there."

He used his keycard to open the door and Mike stepped inside. Everything looked to be the same as he'd seen it before. Her briefcase sat on the bed and her makeup bag was still on the bathroom counter. Only, she wasn't there.

"When was the last time she used her keycard?"

"I called down to the front desk and had someone verify. The last time she used her keycard was yesterday afternoon."

Now he was worried. "She didn't use it last night?" He glanced around at the room, hoping for some indication that she'd been there last night, but nothing stood out. She had definitely been there when he'd phoned her from the hospital, yet she'd never returned.

"No. The only access to the room was yesterday afternoon at two when housekeeping entered to refresh the towels then when she entered around seven."

"You have cameras on the parking lot, right? I need to see them."

He knew she'd gotten another rental car but he had no idea what kind of vehicle it was. They headed to the main office and Steve pulled up the surveillance video. Since it seemed she hadn't made it back to her hotel room last night, Mike had him check the feeds for the hour or so after she'd left him at the hospital. At first, it seemed that she'd never even made it to the hotel but then he spotted the rental car turn into the lot.

"There she is." He saw her in the driver's seat as she pulled into a parking space and got out. She dropped her keys then reached down to get them. His heart stopped as he spotted a figure sneak up behind her. His instinct was to call out to her to warn her but he held his tongue. It wouldn't do any good now. The man grabbed her and held something over her face for several moments as she struggled. Her knees buckled then he forced her into the car before climbing into the driver's seat. The car took off a moment later and headed south down the main road.

"What's the time stamp on that?" he asked.

"One fifty-six this morning."

It was now after ten. Nine hours. He'd had her for nine hours.

While Mike had been stewing about their blowup, she'd spent the evening possibly fighting for her life.

He just prayed he wasn't too late to rescue her.

Mike alerted the sheriff about Christy's abduction and the video evidence to back it up and then collected the video footage for the IT department to review. Hopefully, Jana Carter, their IT expert, could enhance the video so the assailant's face was clearer.

He put out a BOLO on both her and her missing rental vehicle then went to the hospital to see his cousin. He needed to know once and for all from Cliff that he wasn't involved.

Thankfully, Rebecca was nowhere around when Mike entered.

"Hey, Mike. She's gone down to the cafeteria. I just spoke with Mom who said the girls—"

"I'm not here to check how you're doing, Cliff. Agent Williams is missing."

His face paled and he shifted in the bed. "Missing?"

"Someone grabbed her last night before she made it to her hotel room. Do you know anything about that, Cliff?"

His eyes narrowed in anger. "No, I don't. Now you're going to try to accuse me of that too? I can't catch a break."

"I know you weren't responsible for abducting her. I'd say your alibi is airtight. You were confined to a hospital bed with a guard at your door. I just want you to tell me if someone is acting on your behalf. Would one of your friends do something like this to try to help your case?"

He shook his head. "No. I don't know, Mike. I doubt it. This isn't good for me, is it? Am I going back to jail?"

Mike grew angry. It was obvious that the only person Cliff was worried about was himself. "How selfish can you be? I just told you that another woman, someone I care deeply about, has been abducted. She might be dead, for all I know. But all you're concerned about is how this will affect you? Everyone in this family—me, your mother, your wife and kids—

we've all been fighting for you all these years, Cliff. Your family has been the one suffering for your drinking and brawling and you don't care about anyone but yourself. That's just great."

He seemed to get through to his cousin, who stared at him wide-eyed in surprise.

"Once and for all, were you involved in Dawn's disappearance?"

He shook his head. "No. I loved her. I didn't want us to break up, but I would have never killed her, Mike."

"Not even by accident?"

"No. I didn't even see her that night."

"How did you get the gun wound?"

"I did it myself. I was thinking about ending my life and the gun went off accidentally."

He breathed a sigh of relief that at least he had a plausible explanation.

"And I'm not involved in Agent Williams's disappearance either. I don't have people in my life who would want to help me."

"You're full of it, Cliff. You've got people who care about you. You've got a wife and kids who adore you and your friends Jerry and Devon would do most anything for you. But all you can see is your own pain. You don't care about others. I used to envy you, Cliff. I envied the family that you had, wishing I'd grown up with a mother who loved me and a beautiful wife and kids, but you blew it. You never appreciated all you had. You tossed it all away for another bottle of booze."

That was it. He'd had enough. He was through with worrying about Cliff.

He had more important things to do...like finding out what had happened to the woman he had fallen in love with.

Her head was pounding as Christy slowly regained consciousness. She didn't know where she was and, for a moment, couldn't recall what had happened to her. Slowly, it returned. The attack from behind. The abduction. A cloth over her mouth and nose. She recognized the ether smell. He'd dosed her with chloroform.

She pulled at her arms, only to find them tied together to something, although her feet were free. A gag prevented her from calling out for help. The faint light of a window allowed her to see that she was locked inside a small bathroom and that her hands were tied with wire to the plumbing beneath the sink mounted to the wall.

The door, however, was within reach of her legs, which were unbound. She kicked at it several times until it gave and flew open, revealing an office with a desk and a couch. She recognized it immediately. She'd been there before while interviewing Rance Weaver about his towing records.

Anger burned through her that she'd believed him when he'd said he was on the other side of town the night Dawn had vanished and hadn't suspected anything about him until she'd seen Mrs. Langford's reaction to the very mention of his name.

She had no idea how long she'd been unconscious but the window showed it was light outside. It had been dark when she'd been jumped in the hotel parking lot. Surely, by now, Mike would have realized she was missing and started a search for her.

Mike.

Her face warmed with shame at how she'd spoken to him last night. His empathy and goodness were indicative of his good nature yet she'd accused him of covering up a crime. She was embarrassed to have reacted so badly. She'd just wanted answers to her friend's disappearance.

She glanced around the room and realized she was very likely getting the answers she'd spent her life searching for.

Why else would Rance Weaver abduct her and tie her up inside his bathroom? He had to have been involved in Dawn's disappearance. Had he come upon her on the road like Mr. Langford had stated he did sometimes? She'd found no evidence of a criminal record or history of violence against women except for his possible involvement in his sister-in-law's and brother's deaths. Yet Amber Middleton's story had showed her an entirely different view of him.

She pulled at the wires, attempting to free her hands, but they only dug into her wrists and broke the skin. She didn't know for certain what or why Rance Weaver had abducted her, but she needed to escape before he came back to show her.

She tried pulling again but the wire rubbed her skin raw and blood pooled around it. She turned to use her feet to try to kick out the pipes below the sink, to no avail. Finally, she gave up. She was trapped here until Rance returned.

A noise grabbed her attention. Footsteps moving around outside. Suddenly, the door to the building opened and Rance Weaver walked inside. He spotted the open bathroom door and shook his head.

"Trying to escape, are you? That won't happen." He neared her and grabbed her legs, pin-ning them with his body while he loosened the gag on her mouth.

"Why am I here?" she demanded when she could speak. "What do you want with me?"

He let her legs go then grabbed a chair and straddled it close to the entrance of the bathroom but too far away for her to kick him. He motioned toward her bloody wrists. "You shouldn't keep trying that. You'll cut your hand off if you're not careful."

"Your concern for my safety is noted. What do you want from me?"

"Answers."

"About what?"

"About why you're here in Mercy. What brought you to town, Agent Williams of the FBI?"

She stared at him. Her presence worried him despite the fact that he hadn't even been on her radar until yesterday. *Too bad you didn't abduct me yesterday, Weaver. No one would have been the wiser.*

She decided to be honest with him and, hopefully, he would be honest too. "I came to Mercy to find out what happened to Dawn Cafferty. She disappeared twelve years ago on her way home from college. But you knew that, didn't you? You broke into my hotel room and found out. You tried to threaten me into leaving, too, but it didn't work. Do you remember Dawn? Did you abduct her too?"

He didn't respond, didn't even flinch at the mention of her name. "Why do you care about her? That case has been cold for over a decade."

"Because I knew her. We went to school together. She was my friend. You killed her, didn't you, Rance?"

He ignored her question and she saw the truth in his eyes. Some perpetrators might spill their guts and confess knowing that she was never going to make it out of this building alive, but he wasn't even going to do that. He didn't care that she wanted to know and certainly didn't seem ready to tell her the truth.

Tires squealed outside. Weaver tensed and walked to the window, peeking through the blind. He swore then kicked the chair aside as he hurried to her, bound her feet with duct tape then replaced the gag on her mouth.

"Don't make a sound," he commanded, which keyed her in that someone was outside and he was worried about them finding a woman tied up in his bathroom.

She couldn't risk not trying to get their attention. It might be Mike here to search for her.

Even if it wasn't, this person might be her only hope of living through this abduction.

She cried out, her screams muffled by the gag. In response, Weaver turned and kicked her hard in the stomach, sending pain radiating through her and her struggling to catch her breath. He rammed his fist into her, as well, then shoved her completely into the bathroom and slammed the door.

All she could think of was the pain even as she knew she had to fight through it to save her own life.

Rance slammed the front door hard enough to shake the building. She heard a car door slam then angry words grow louder between Rance and someone else. It sounded like the fight was growing ugly. She caught her breath then pushed through the pain to try to raise her head enough to see through a small corner of the window. A man with a baseball bat was swinging it and yelling at Rance.

Langford. It was Chris Langford.

She tapped on the pipes, hoping to grab his attention even while knowing there was no way he would hear her over the yelling between them.

She heard the wail of a siren then lights that

indicated the sheriff's office had arrived. Her heart soared.

Mike had found her.

She banged louder and tried to yell, but the commotion outside was loud too. She stretched her neck to see what was happening and saw another deputy, not Mike, separating the two men then placing them both into the back seat of his vehicle.

Christy's heart fell as the cruiser drove away without her. The deputy hadn't even searched the property. He hadn't been there looking for her, which told her Mike had no idea where she was.

She turned away from the window and pulled at the wires around her hands again. She had to get free and get out of there before Rance Weaver returned.

ELEVEN

Steve was busy at the front desk when Mike arrived at the hotel. "I authorized a keycard for you," he said, handing it over. "All I ask is that you return it before you leave."

He agreed and hurried upstairs to Christy's room. He unlocked the door then glanced around, zeroing in on her laptop. That was what he'd come after. He picked it up then took out his cell phone to let Jana know he'd found it and was on the way back to the sheriff's office to give it to her. He was praying she could find something on Christy's computer that would give them a clue as to who had taken her.

"I'll be waiting," Jana told him. "I've finished going through the hotel's video feed. I've done everything I know to enhance the image, but I can't get enough to make facial recognition possible. Sorry, Mike."

It was a letdown but he wasn't giving up. "What about sending it to the FBI lab? Have

Sheriff Thompson call over there. Maybe they have more advanced technology."

She sighed and agreed to try. "Don't hold your breath, though. The hoodie this guy is wearing is obstructing his face. Even the FBI won't be able to overcome that obstacle."

Without being able to identify her abductor, they were left to scour through the evidence of the case to try to figure out who had taken her. Cliff was out, since he was confined to the hospital, but they still didn't know who had been targeting her or why.

He returned the keycard to Steve and sped to the sheriff's office with the laptop.

The squad room was chaos when he returned as Deputy Gordon led two men into the building. They were shouting threats back and forth at one another and each showed bruises and signs of a fight. Mike spotted a bat in an evidence bag. Obviously, the confrontation had gotten ugly.

He was surprised to realize he knew both men. Rance Weaver and Chris Langford. He and Christy had interviewed both of them on Dawn's case. He didn't recall Langford showing any ill feelings toward Weaver at the time despite him taking his calls occasionally, so this level of animosity surprised him.

"What's going on?" he asked Deputy Gordon as he parked Langford in an interview room and cuffed him to the table.

Gordon stepped out of the room before answering him. "We got a call from Langford's wife that he was out of his mind with anger and heading over to confront Weaver. When I arrived, he was beating Weaver with that baseball bat. Kept shouting at him and calling him names. So, I brought them both in. Weaver declined to go to the hospital so I brought him here to get his statement. I was hoping, after a few minutes, they would both calm down, but things got pretty ugly."

Mike glanced at Weaver, who was now sitting beside Gordon's desk pressing a paper towel to his bleeding lip. "I wonder what started it."

"I don't know yet, but Langford's wife is on her way in too. He seems to have been the instigator. For right now, I'm going to give Langford time to cool off while I take Weaver's statement."

"Is Weaver going to file charges?"

Gordon shrugged. "Who knows? He really didn't want to come in and give a statement, but I insisted. I'll take it down then drive him back home. By then, Langford should be settled down enough to tell me what happened. You want to assist me?"

Mike was curious about this dustup but he couldn't devote any time to helping Gordon when Christy was missing. Her safety was his first priority. "I can't, sorry." He held up the laptop. "Jana's waiting on this."

He hurried down the hallway toward Jana's office and delivered the laptop, praying she could get something from it, but he was doubtful. They hadn't made any big breakthroughs on the case so he wasn't expecting to find anything on it. Still, he was covering all of his bases.

"I'll get right on this," Jana promised him. "I sent the video feed to the FBI lab. They were happy to help, especially once they learned it was one of their own who'd been abducted. However, the tech I spoke with agreed with me about the obstruction, Mike. It's doubtful we'll get an identification from it." She touched the laptop. "Maybe something on here will be fruitful, though."

"I hope so." He was running out of ideas about how to find her and time was running out.

Sheriff Thompson hurried up to him, holding a slip of paper in her hand. "We just received a call from the rental company where Agent Williams rented her vehicle."

He'd called them earlier about GPS coordinates for Christy's rental car. "And?"

"They've located the vehicle. It's in their lot."

So someone had returned her car to the rental company. "Did they see who returned it?"

"No. It was dropped off and the key left in the ignition."

"Well, they must have cameras."

She shook her head. "I asked that, of course. The car was left in an area where there were no direct angles, but we might be able to see it from peripheral cameras. They're pulling them up now. Also, it's not at the store here in Mercy. It's in the London location."

London was a small town in the next county. So, whoever had dropped off her car must have been closer to the next county than to town.

"Call them back right now and tell them not to touch the vehicle. I'm on my way with a team to process it."

The sheriff handed the paper to another deputy with instructions to phone them. "I'm coming with you," she said, turning back to Mike.

He didn't argue because he didn't have time to worry about hierarchies and also because he was glad not to be on this alone. He'd grown used to having someone by his side. To having Christy by his side. "Thank you."

She nodded. "The FBI entrusted Agent Williams to our town. Nothing is going to happen to her on my watch. Let's go."

They made the forty-five-minute drive to the next county followed by another two-man team to collect any evidence in the vehicle. They found the rental company and parked. The manager hurried out to greet them then led them to the back parking area and to the rental car. Mike hadn't been with Christy when she'd rented this car after her other rental had been totaled, so he didn't recognize it except from seeing it on the black-and-white video surveillance from the hotel.

"Has anyone messed with the car?" Mike asked him.

The manager shook his head. "No. We received a call from the office in Mercy saying the GPS had indicated the car was here. I came out and looked and there she was. Someone returned it and must have parked it out here so we wouldn't realize it. We didn't even know the car was here until the other location phoned."

Whomever had left it here had obviously been hoping to have the car fade in with the other vehicles on the lot. That indicated a desire to hide it for as long as possible.

Bile rose in his throat as he slipped on gloves

then opened the car door. Christy's perfume hit him in the face and nearly made his knees buckle. This was the last place he knew she'd been. Paperwork, a water bottle, a phone charger and pack of tissues sat on the passenger seat. He knew most of her stuff was still back at the hotel, so there wasn't much of it in here. He glanced around but didn't see blood or any evidence that something violent had happened inside the car. But just because he didn't see it didn't mean it wasn't there. He hit the button that popped open the trunk then climbed from the car, bracing himself for what he might find when he opened it.

Sheriff Thompson looked tense, as well, as he circled to the back of the car. "Do you want me to look?"

"No, I'll do it." They both knew what he was looking for as he walked to the rear of the vehicle and pulled open the trunk.

A rush of relief hit him at seeing it was empty.

He'd been afraid of finding her body inside. That didn't mean she hadn't been in there at some point, but he would leave that determination to the crime scene team.

He waved them over. "Let's check the car for evidence. We know we're going to find Agent

Williams's prints and hairs on the driver's side. Let's see what else we find."

Someone had driven it here and dropped it off, doing their best not to be seen, but that meant they'd left forensic evidence in the car as well. He hoped it might lead him to whomever had taken Christy because he knew she hadn't left town on her own. He had video evidence of that.

And wherever she was, he prayed she was still alive.

Sheriff Thompson questioned the workers at the rental center, but no one seemed to know anything. They checked the security footage, which did capture the vehicle pulling into the lot and then a figure fleeing. Only, the darkness hid the driver's identity. Thanks to the video, they now knew several key details—someone had parked the car at four-fifteen in the morning, that he'd fled the lot on foot, and that Christy had not been with him.

Mike grit his teeth, unwilling to think about what that might mean for her.

Sheriff Thompson's cell phone rang and she stepped out to take it. She returned moments later with news. "Jana phoned. She found something on the laptop she wants us to see."

His pulse kicked up a notch. Finally, progress. He instructed the manager to forward a copy of that footage to Jana's email. Hopefully, she could work her expertise on it and find something that they'd missed.

"Has the crime scene team found anything?" Sheriff Thompson asked him as they hurried outside.

"They found a few hairs and some touch DNA, but there wasn't much. They'll follow us back to the office once they've completed going through it."

They climbed into the SUV and headed toward Mercy. "Did Jana say what it was she found?"

"Some kind of notes about the investigation. She said they were time-dated yesterday, so perhaps she found something that pointed to her abductor."

He couldn't imagine what it was. He'd been searching for his cousin most of the day then dealing with his crisis. Christy had been on her own all day, so there was no telling what she'd found in spite of the fact she hadn't mentioned anything to him at the hospital. Then again, they hadn't exactly been on the best terms at that moment.

Shame filled him at how he'd spoken to her

and his greatest fear at the moment was that those might be the last words he ever said to her.

He didn't want it to end that way between them. He gripped the steering wheel tighter. *God, please help us find her.*

Sheriff Thompson must have noticed his pain because she reassured him. "We'll find her, Mike. We won't stop until we do."

They made it back to the sheriff's office and met Jana in her office.

"What did you find?" Sheriff Thompson asked her.

"These notes were made yesterday. They talk about her discovering that Rance Weaver has a history of attacking women when he picks them up in his tow truck."

"What? His record didn't show anything like that. Plus, we interviewed him. He wasn't even on the right side of town the night Dawn vanished."

Jana shared the laptop screen with the notes via the big screen on the wall. "She addressed that too. There was a victim, Amber Middleton, sixteen at the time. Agent Williams interviewed her mother, Joanna, yesterday. Apparently, her car broke down and her parents called for a tow truck. Rance Weaver showed up instead. He loaded up her vehicle then had her get into his truck, where he assaulted her. She managed to escape the cab of the truck and the family pressed charges against him."

"That wasn't on his rap sheet," Mike insisted.

"It was. Only the prosecutor pled it down to a misdemeanor assault. He was sentenced to community service."

Understanding dawned on Mike. "And because they pled it without the sexual component, he didn't have to register as a sex offender, so he didn't show up on our sweep."

Amber Middleton hadn't gotten any real justice for her attack. Weaver should have done time for the assault, but that wasn't for him to say. At least, he'd been charged and had pleaded guilty. Only, as part of the plea agreement, he hadn't had to register as a sex offender. That had kept him off the sheriff's office's radar for years and hadn't been a red flag to the investigation to look closer at him.

"Why didn't this incident come up when we were looking for older cases that matched the Cafferty case?" Sheriff Thompson asked him. "You ran his sheet."

He shook his head. "It's one isolated incident. It happened eight years after Dawn vanished and on the opposite side of town. Plus, Amber Middleton wasn't killed. She didn't vanish. She survived and pressed charges. My guess is that no one connected it to Dawn's given the time between them. Also, since he didn't have to register as a sex offender as part of his plea bargain, he didn't come up when we ran the sex offender registry."

"I assume Agent Williams suspected Weaver might be connected to Dawn's disappearance?"

"That seems to be the path she was on," Jana confirmed. "She even reinterviewed Tony Freely and gave him a photo lineup that included Weaver and your cousin, Mike. According to her notes, Freely couldn't say for certain after seeing Weaver's photo that it wasn't him and not your cousin."

Mike leaned against the desk and tried to process everything. Christy had done, all of this while he'd been searching for his cousin. Why hadn't she mentioned these new findings to him at the hospital? This new evidence didn't clear Cliff, but it did seem to point to Weaver being involved.

"Rance Weaver owns that junkyard near the county line, doesn't he?" Sheriff Thompson asked.

Mike nodded. A junkyard was a perfect place to hide a body and dispose of someone's vehicle. And he'd just been here at the sheriff's office just hours ago.

Mike hurried into the squad room and found Gordon. "Where's Rance Weaver? Is he still here?"

Gordon shook his head. "No, I had Deputy Morgan drive him back to his garage."

"Call him," Mike insisted. "Tell him to turn around and bring Weaver back, but not to tell him why."

Gordon picked up the phone and made the call.

"He's not answering his cell phone," Gordon commented after several rings went unanswered. "He has a bad habit of putting it silent. Do you want me to try him on the radio?"

"No," Sheriff Thompson said, stopping him.

Mike turned to her. "We have to go. He could be holding her there." He'd already disposed of her car. How long did she have before he disposed of her? He couldn't let his mind even go there.

"We have no probable cause. Nothing directly indicates Weaver was involved in Agent Williams's abduction. Unless he consents—"

"Which he won't," Mike insisted.

"—we don't have enough evidence to get a

warrant to search the grounds," Sheriff Thompson finished.

Mike slammed his hand against the desk. This was their first real lead and they couldn't go in because of a search warrant. He thought about Weaver sitting here at the sheriff's office, probably laughing at them all, knowing he had Christy and they'd had no idea.

"We can't just sit here and do nothing, Sheriff."

"We're not doing nothing. Gordon, go track down Morgan and join him. We can't step foot on Weaver's property without a warrant, but that doesn't mean we can't keep an eye on the place. If you observe anything suspicious or see Agent Williams, call it in."

"Will do, Sheriff," Gordon said before gathering his things and hurrying out of the building.

Sheriff Thompson continued. "I'll go put a fire under the lab on that evidence from the rental car. Maybe he left his fingerprints inside it."

Mike remembered Weaver had been brought in along with Chris Langford for fighting. He suddenly wanted to know everything about what had happened between them.

He checked the interview room and saw Langford was still inside, along with his wife. Mike entered the room and both of them looked up.

"I need to know what you and Rance Weaver were fighting about," he told Langford.

He leaned back in his seat. "After Agent Williams came to see us yesterday, I finally convinced my wife to tell me what Weaver did to her. I guess I lost my cool and confronted him."

She backed up his story. "He just lost it and took off, saying he was going to give Weaver what was coming to him. I called the sheriff's office to go there because I was worried what he might do."

He looked at Mrs. Langford. "So this all started when you told Agent Williams about something Rance Weaver did to you?"

She lowered her head, embarrassed, then looked at her husband before nodding.

"Now, why don't you tell me what Weaver did to you?"

He didn't want to think about the terrible thing that had happened to her, but he hoped her statement would be enough to get a warrant for Rance Weaver and find out if he'd had anything to do with Christy's abduction.

"She's already given a statement to Agent Williams," Chris Langford insisted. "Why does she have to repeat it again?"

Mike decided honesty was the best policy here. "Agent Williams is missing. Someone abducted her last night. We believe it was Weaver but, so far, we haven't been able to prove it."

They both looked stunned for a moment then Langford grew thoughtful. "You know, when I first got out of my truck to approach Weaver, I could have sworn I saw something, movement, in a window. It sounded like someone was trying to call out for help." He pulled a hand through his hair as his face reddened with shame. "But I was so intent on confronting Weaver that I didn't give it a second thought. And when I even mentioned something about it, he came unglued and started yelling at me to get off his property or I'd be sorry."

Mike's pulse raced with excitement at this new information. "Are you sure?"

He locked eyes with Mike. "Someone was in there."

Mike hurried out to share this new piece of evidence with the sheriff. His heart was pounding with excitement. If Langford was right, that was proof that Christy had been alive as of an hour ago. It was also all the probable cause they needed to get a warrant to search Weaver's property.

* * *

Christy continued to pull at the binds around her hands and tried kicking at the pipes. She had no idea how long she'd been doing so, but it seemed like hours had passed since the sheriff's office had taken Weaver away. Had they arrested him for her abduction? No. They would be looking for her if they had and she wasn't exactly hidden well. All they had to do was enter the building or even walk around it for her to be seen.

Lord, please help me get out of this.

Her face warmed that she was reaching out to God for help, but she had no idea when Weaver would return. When he did, she was certain he was going to kill her. Knowing he wasn't even a suspect of the sheriff's office would only embolden him. She would disappear as surely and completely as her friend had done.

She kicked again and again at the pipes below the sink, praying they would give. It was her only way out. They didn't budge. Finally, she collapsed, tears streaming down her face. She didn't want to die like this. She wasn't ready for this to be the end.

Christy wanted another chance to apologize to Mike and to tell him how much she cared about him…how much she'd grown to love him. He really was the best person she'd ever known. His kindness and compassion were unmatched and it wasn't often she met a man she could depend on to do the right thing.

And he trusted in God.

If someone like Mike could trust Him, then she could too.

She'd kept God at arm's length since Dawn had gone missing, blaming him for allowing her friend to disappear. An all-knowing God would know where Dawn was. Why hadn't He revealed her location to someone? And she was about to follow in Dawn's wake. How long would it be before someone discovered her? Another twelve years? Even longer?

Tires on gravel pulled her away from her thoughts of death. She strained to see through the window and saw a sheriff's office cruiser pull in close to the building. The passenger door opened and Weaver got out.

Now was her chance to draw attention to herself. She screamed as loudly as her muffled gag would allow her and pounded her feet against the wall, praying that the deputy in the driver's seat would hear a commotion and investigate.

It was her only hope of surviving.

She kept pounding away and trying to call attention to herself until the cruiser left. Hot tears pressed against her eyes as all hope faded for her rescue. She listened to footsteps approaching the building then the door opening and closing and those same footsteps moving toward the bathroom where she lay. She turned herself over and moved as close to the wall as possible. Not that it would do any good. The door swung open and Weaver stood over her, grinning smugly.

He reached into his pocket and pulled out a knife. "I hope that proves to you that no one is coming looking for you," he said as he leaned over her and cut the wire from the pipes then yanked her to her feet. "No one is looking for you," he told her. "I was there at the sheriff's office and no one even cared that you were missing."

Her face burned with anger, knowing he was lying. Mike would definitely be looking for her. He might not have figured out that Weaver was behind her disappearance, but he would eventually. He was a good investigator.

Weaver picked her up and tossed her over his shoulder then carried her outside through the junkyard land of abandoned cars. The acreage was massive and it was nearly bumper-to-bumper with old cars and parts lying around. He walked to an old model, opened the trunk then dumped her into it.

"Even if you manage to get that gag off and call for help, no one is around for miles to hear you," he told her. "Say hello to your friend Dawn for me when you see her," he told her arrogantly before slamming the trunk lid and leaving her in darkness. He wasn't even going to kill her. He was just going to leave her to die, trapped in this car in the hot sun.

Fear rustled through her but it wasn't a fear of death. She wasn't afraid of dying but afraid of what she was leaving behind. Mike and a wonderful future with him. It pained her to think what might have been. And how he would blame himself that he couldn't keep her safe.

Jesus, please be with him. I love him so much.

What she wouldn't give for another opportunity to tell him so.

TWELVE

"We've got the warrant," Sheriff Thompson said as she stepped into the tactical room where Mike and the other deputies were prepping for the raid on Weaver's property. "Mr. Langford's first-hand statement about seeing someone was enough for the judge to authorize the search."

"Good." He'd been prepared to go in without one if it meant a chance to save Christy, but having the warrant meant less of a chance for Weaver to wrangle a way out of the criminal offenses he was soon to be charged with.

They gathered together with a map of Rance Weaver's property, where Josh had laid out a plan to surround and search the property, giving everyone on the team an assigned area.

"Mike, you'll approach him first for security purposes. Sheriff Thompson will present the warrant then take Weaver into custody and then the rest of us will spread out and start the search for Agent Williams. It makes sense he might be keeping her in one of the vehicles on the property, so we'll have to search them all, but there's also several sheds, a garage and a wooded area that connects to his acreage. We'll have to search that too."

Mike was itching to get going. He had no idea where Christy was and a lot of time had passed. Something terrible could have happened to her. He couldn't allow his mind to go down that path. He had to remain optimistic. Whatever they found at that junkyard, Rance Weaver's days of freedom would soon be over.

"Let's get going," Josh told them all and everyone loaded up.

Mike rode with another deputy. His heart was racing and he was nervous about what they might find when they arrived. Only the knowledge that God was still in control, even when things looked bleak, gave him any peace.

Lord, please keep her safe until I can find her.

Josh instructed several deputies to set up along the perimeter and watch and wait until they approached Rance. Everyone got out then Josh gave Mike, who had been assigned the duty of approaching Weaver, the signal to go. He walked to the front of the building and rang the bell then knocked on the door. No one answered and he didn't hear movement from inside. He glanced through the windows and noted the desk overturned and stuff strewn on the floors. If Christy had been there before, as Langford had claimed, she wasn't there now.

"No one's there, but it looks like something happened."

Josh circled the front of the property and the side before returning. "There's a truck parked under a canopy on the other side of the building, so it's possible he's still somewhere on the property." He glanced at Mike. "It matches the description of the truck that ran Agent Williams off the road, plus there's damage to it."

That was enough to implicate him in the attack against her.

Sheriff Thompson took in this information then nodded. "Deputies Gordon and Morgan have been watching the property and didn't see him leave so, unless he left before they arrived, he's still here. Only we don't need him to be here to execute the warrant. But make sure to tell everyone to be watchful in case we run across him."

Josh clicked on his radio and relayed the message to the group.

Mike was glad the sheriff had made the call that they weren't waiting for Weaver to show up. They didn't need to since they had the warrant in hand. Good.

Josh walked to the fence and peeked through then called for someone to cut the padlock on the gate. A deputy arrived with a large pair of bolt cutters. Mike raised his rifle and entered through the fence along with everyone else as Josh pulled it open. They spread out, the sheriff and a small group remaining behind in case Weaver returned. If he did, she would show him the warrant then take him into custody.

The junkyard was full of old cars for rows. It was a perfect place to hide.

Josh motioned for the team to spread out and search in their preassigned grids. They didn't know where Weaver was but they had to assume he was armed and dangerous given his known previous attacks. Mike hurried to his grid and began checking each car systematically. He was hyperfocused on searching the property but, so far, they saw no sign of Weaver or Christy.

Suddenly, movement from the woods grabbed his attention. He spotted Weaver heading back into the yard, a shovel in his hands. He raised his weapon. "Don't move," he shouted.

Weaver spotted him then turned and darted back into the trees.

"I've got Weaver running into the woods," Mike called over the radio. "I'm in pursuit."

Mike chased after him and Josh and several deputies followed.

Josh was talking into the radio. "Surround the property. Don't let him get past you."

Mike hopped over the fence and chased Weaver into a clearing, where he dropped the shovel and pulled out a gun.

"Don't move, Weaver," Mike yelled at him, but he responded by raising the gun in his hand. Mike fired in response, hitting him. He clutched his shoulder as the gun fell from his hand and he dropped to his knees.

Josh and several deputies caught up and rushed over to him. Josh kicked Weaver's gun away and another deputy grabbed the shovel. Josh leaned over him then looked back at Mike.

"He's alive." He pressed his hand onto Weaver's shoulder wound to stop the bleeding then radioed for an ambulance. "Looks like he's got a couple more gunshot wounds too. One to the hand and one to the side."

That confirmed that he'd been the one to ambush Christy. Mike stood over the man he'd just shot. He could see he was in pain, but Mike had other concerns. He knelt beside him. "Where's Agent Williams?"

"I don't know."

"I know you abducted her just like you did Dawn and those other women. Now, where is she?"

Weaver grimaced in pain but didn't answer.

Deputy Gordon ran up a hill then returned a moment later. "There's freshly overturned dirt up the hill."

Josh tipped his head at Mike. "Go check. I've got him."

He wasn't sure his legs would move at the thought that he might be finding where Weaver had buried Christy, but he forced himself to move and hurried up the hill after Gordon. When he arrived, he saw that the mound of dirt didn't look large enough for a body.

Gordon started digging and soon unearthed a small sack. He pulled it out. It contained several items, including Christy's phone and FBI identification badge.

He got on the radio. "We found items belonging to Agent Williams but not her."

Josh responded. "If you don't see any other dig sites, let's continue checking the cars."

Mike turned to Deputy Gordon, who shook his head. "I didn't see any other sites that he might have been digging in."

Mike rubbed his face, realizing that Gordon

was right. Why bury a body when he could easily dispose of it in one of the hundreds of cars he had on the lot. "Let's get back to searching. She has to be here somewhere."

He rushed down the hill to where Josh was still covering Weaver.

"Where is she?" he demanded of Weaver. "What did you do with Agent Williams?"

Weaver looked at Mike and his eyes were cold. "You'll never find her."

Mike glanced at Josh then called out to everyone. "Spread out and search the cars. She has to be inside one of them."

Josh agreed. "I doubt he would take her off the property. This is his safe haven and he knows we can't search it without a warrant. He probably never thought we would be able to obtain one."

Mike glared at him then tossed the bag with her phone and credentials inside. "He thought wrong. That's enough to convict him. Read him his rights then get him out of here."

Mike hurried back to the yard to search the cars. Josh had been right about one thing. This was Weaver's own personal space and he protected it. This had to be where he'd hidden Christy. He just prayed he wasn't too late to find her.

He called out her name. They were looking at a sea of cars that stretched as far as he could see. She could be hidden in or beneath any one of them and, given the hot sun barreling down on them, if she was still alive, her time was limited. He tried not to panic, but the thought of losing her was more than he could bear.

It was unthinkable to him that he'd fallen for her so quickly and so completely, yet he had, and the thought of being without her nearly destroyed him. He didn't know if she felt the same about him but he hoped she did and he desperately wanted the chance to find out.

She was a fighter. If she was alive and able, she would do what she could to help them locate her.

"Christy! Christy, can you hear me?"

He listened, hoping for a cry for help or a pinging sound to help him locate her, but there was nothing.

"Spread out," he told the team. "Check every car."

He frantically searched. He had to find her.

"Here!" Deputy Stokes hollered. "I found something."

Mike's gut clenched as he hurried over. He saw Stokes standing behind a car with the trunk open, but he wasn't pulling anyone out. That wasn't a good sign. Was she already dead?

He hurried to the deputy's position, bracing himself for the worst, only to breathe a sigh of relief when he saw what Stokes was calling about. He had found someone, but not Christy. This body was nothing but skeletal remains. Years old. He was possibly looking at Dawn's body or one of the other missing women. The car didn't match the one Dawn had been driving, but that didn't mean it wasn't her.

It did mean it was a good chance that if he'd stuffed one woman into trunk of a car, he'd probably done the same to Christy.

"Call in the crime scene techs and the coroner. The rest of us will continue searching."

He heard the call as Stokes put the word out on the radio that they'd found a body. He watched as Josh walked Weaver through the yard in handcuffs. Mike glared at him and noticed a smirk on his face. He didn't know if he'd heard the call about the body, but Weaver could now be charged with murder once they identified who the remains belonged to.

Mike kept checking cars. His mind was whirling with anxiety yet he did his best to focus all his energy on finding Christy. He slammed one car door after another futile search and then stopped, knelt and lowered his head.

Lord, guide my steps.

A sound grabbed his attention. It was faint, but he heard it once he stopped being so frantic. It was a faint tapping on metal.

He called out for everyone to be quiet and strained his ears to listen. "Do you hear that?" he asked the others, who also strained to listen.

He zeroed in on the noise and followed it to an old beater with a crushed front end. "Here!" he called. He ran to the car and pounded on it. "Christy, are you in there?"

He didn't wait for an answer. He grabbed the crowbar and broke the lock then opened the trunk. His heart fell into his stomach when he saw her, unmoving, except for her hand that was slowly tapping on the inside metal with something in her fingers. Her wrists were bleeding from the wire wrapped around them, her feet were bound and she was gagged.

"I've got you," he said as he grabbed behind her neck and knees and pulled her out of the hot trunk.

He loosened the gag on her mouth and pushed it down. Her lips were chapped and she was severely weak, probably from being inside that hot trunk for who knew how long. Weaver had left her there to die from exposure.

He touched his radio. "I found her. I need an ambulance. Hurry."

He placed her on the ground and a deputy hurried to offer her a bottle of water. He opened it and gently poured some over her lips. She drank it but coughed and gagged when it was too much.

"Weaver." She'd whispered the warning but he did his best to reassure her.

"He's in custody. He can't hurt you or anyone else again. Are you injured?" he asked, checking her out. He didn't see any noticeable injuries aside from the raw skin from the wires.

Another deputy hurried over with a small pair of handheld wire cutters and handed them to Mike. He gently cut the binds at her hands and feet, causing her to cry out in pain as they rubbed her open wounds.

"It's going to be okay," he assured her.

Once she was free, she threw her arms around his neck. He pressed her against him, so thankful she was safe and alive.

"You really got him?" she asked and he nodded.

"I saw him marched off in cuffs myself. I'm just sorry I wasn't the one to arrest him."

She pressed against him, clinging to him. "I knew you would look for me," she whispered. "I knew you wouldn't let me go."

He touched her face as he shook his head and made her a promise. "Never."

She tried to smile at that then grimaced as her lips cracked. Sorrow filled her eyes. "He didn't confess. He wouldn't confess to me that he killed Dawn. Even after all this, I can't prove he did anything to her."

"That probably won't matter. We found remains while we were searching for you. It might be Dawn's or it might be someone else's, but it implicates him in murder. He's going to prison for a long, long time."

"Take me there. I want to see."

She tried to stand up. He helped her and let her lean on him as he walked her over to the car where they'd found the skeletal remains.

She glanced into the trunk and her chin quivered. She dug her face into his chest. "It's Dawn."

"How can you tell?" It was possible she was only hoping, and he would understand that, but she insisted.

"The earrings. I was with her when she bought them. She was wearing them the day she left school."

He spotted a pair of ladybug earrings near the skull. That detail hadn't been listed in the missing person's report, but Christy would have known it. Mike suddenly flashed back to the night he'd pulled her over. She'd pushed a strand of hair behind her ear and he'd seen those earrings. He was glad to know they'd found her. They would have to wait on the official verification before they could charge Weaver for her murder, but Christy's identification was good enough for him.

"The forensic team is here," Deputy Stokes told him, motioning to the white van that had arrived and the personnel embarking.

"Okay. Let's get out of their way and let them do their jobs." He led Christy away, but he wasn't going to let her out of his sight again.

He leaned over her and touched her hair, relief flooding through him. "I was so worried about you. I thought I'd lost you." He bent down and kissed her, and she clung to him.

"I thought you had too." Her voice was raspy and full of emotion. "I'm sorry for what I said the last time we spoke," she told him.

He waved her apology away. "I don't care about that. All I care is that you're safe. I couldn't think of anything else except getting to you." Her touched her face. "I love you,

Christy. I've fallen hopelessly and helplessly in love with you."

She did her best to smile again, but shook her head. "Not hopelessly, Mike. We have hope in God. I had hope that you would find me and you did." She leaned up and kissed him. "I love you too."

And now that he had her back, he was never letting her go again.

EPILOGUE

Mike kept his arm around Christy's shoulder as the preacher finished up the eulogy. It was a beautiful day for the long-awaited funeral for Dawn. Dental records had confirmed Christy's initial identification that the bones they'd found in the car at Weaver's belonged to her friend. The case was finally closed for good.

Many people in the community who had known Dawn and her family had showed up to pay their respects. Mr. and Mrs. Cafferty looked weary, but Christy knew they were relieved to finally have this moment. Years earlier, they'd erected a tombstone for their daughter, but today they had her body to bury there and the sought-for closure of finally knowing what had happened to their daughter.

The preacher ended the graveside service and the crowd dispersed.

Mrs. Cafferty saw Christy and headed her way, pulling her into a tight hug. "Thank you.

You brought her home, just as you said you would."

Christy hugged her back tightly. "I was glad to do it."

"I'm just sorry for what happened to you. For what you had to go through."

Christy waved away her concerns. "I'm fine. We found Dawn and that's all that matters." That and that she'd gotten a predator off the street.

"Don't be a stranger. You're welcome here anytime."

She thanked her, though Christy had no plans to return to Mercy. She'd done what she'd come there for. Finding Dawn had been her mission since leaving college and now she wasn't sure what to do with the rest of her life. Go back to the FBI, she supposed, and help other families find the answers they sought.

She touched Mike's hand as it found her shoulder again and realized she did have a reason to come back. They'd proclaimed their love for one another, but she still didn't know where that left them. Staying in Mercy wasn't feasible for her career. The closest FBI field office was hours away and she wasn't ready to give up her career yet. Only, she also couldn't imagine a life without Mike.

He led her over to a bench and they sat down. He'd spent much of the previous day with his family and Christy hadn't had the opportunity to catch up on what was happening with Cliff. She'd received the records she'd subpoenaed for Dawn's Let's Chat messages, but they hadn't offered anything to implicate Cliff. He'd been exonerated on the suspicions that he'd killed Dawn and even on the attacks against her, which Weaver had confessed to, but his life had still taken a turn for the worst recently. "How is your cousin?"

"He's agreed to enter rehab. The family is relieved. They're all relieved to finally have his name cleared and put this mess behind them. I'm hoping he gets the help he needs and that he's ready to get his life back on track."

She smiled. "He has people who care about him, including you."

He reached for her hand and held it. "True, only I can't be the one who holds them all accountable any longer. I can't be." Mike carried the burden of his family on his shoulders and she was glad to see that he was finally being relieved of some of that. "I won't be around to make sure he stays on the straight and narrow. He's going to have to do that on his own."

"What do you mean? Where are you going?"

He stroked her cheek and smiled. "Wherever you're going."

Happiness flooded her but also a bit of uncertainty too. She didn't want to be the one to rip him from his hometown. "Are you sure you want to do that, Mike? Mercy is your home."

"It has been my home and I've loved it here, but now home is wherever you are. I can get a law enforcement job anywhere and, honestly, I just don't want to be here without you." He reached into his pocket and pulled out a ring.

Christy couldn't stop the smile that spread across her face as happiness rolled through her. She was glad he'd made the decision on his own.

"If you'll have me, Christy Williams, I want to ask you to marry me."

Her future suddenly opened up around her. She'd spent her life trying to be a strong, independent woman, but life looked very different to her now than she'd ever imagined. She looked forward to being a wife to Mike, and someday a mother, in addition to being an FBI agent.

She leaned over and kissed him softly. "I would love to be your wife, Mike. I love you."

He smiled then slid the ring on her finger and sealed the deal with a kiss.

This town would always hold a special place in her heart. It was where she'd found her own form of mercy.

* * * * *